PRIZEFIGHT

ADEN LOWE

Enjoy Reading!
Aden Lowe

Author's Note: This book contains adult situations and language, violence, and sexual activity. Mature readers only.

Acknowledgements:

Prizefight wasn't meant to be a book. It was just a short story for a charity anthology. However, like my characters tend to do, Ryker insisted on having his whole story told. The impatient bastard also refused to wait his turn, leaving me no choice but to go ahead and write his book.

This, and my other books, would be impossible without the massive support from my readers. I appreciate each and every one of you, and am incredibly honored that you choose to read my stories. In addition, so many bloggers have posted and shared my posts, cover reveals, teasers, sales, and much more. These amazing people put vast time and energy into promoting authors, and the only pay they get is our thanks. So to all the wonderful bloggers out there, thank you. I appreciate all your effort.

I'm amazed that other authors also share my posts and teasers. Romance authors are some of the kindest, most generous people in the world. I've been fortunate enough to get to know, and become friends with, some super cool ladies. You ladies fucking ROCK, and I'm proud to share your work and have you share mine. I'm not listing, because it's really late as I write this, and I know I would accidentally miss someone. You all know who you are anyway ;)

Ashley Wheels, what can I say? Thank you for keeping my ass out of the fire, LOL. From Assistant, to Baby Sister, to Co-Author, you're the best. You might be a crazy li'l redheaded chick in a wheelchair, but you can do any damn thing you put your mind to. Never forget that, rotten girl.

Tape, you might bust my chops and give me hell about writing "girly shit", but I'm glad to know you've got my back, no matter what comes.

Mom, thanks for NOT reading my books!

Elyse, as always, you're my world. Without you, life would be cold and dark, with no stories worth telling.

Prologue

Ryker:

I stood heaving, catching my breath and sizing up my opponent again. If I didn't find a weakness soon, I was going to get my ass handed to me. The other fighter outweighed me by a good thirty pounds and had a longer reach. Weight divisions were out the window in illegal fights like this. The guy's grin around his mouth-guard said he knew he had me worried.

Well, fuck that. I had too much riding on this match to lose. I just had to find the right advantage and use it. A bright flash of movement outside the cage drew my attention for a split second, reminding me of the complicated prize for this one. Hell, I wasn't even sure I wanted part of it. Still, I had a ranking to maintain, and the money would pay the bills. I focused back on my opponent, replaying every move of the match so far.

The damn girl on the other side of the wire wouldn't stop hopping back and forth, distracting me. Once more I dragged my attention back to the other guy. Suddenly, I saw it. The guy stayed on the front of his right foot. Always. Even when he should have been on his heel. He was doing a very good job at covering a weakness.

Satisfied, I concentrated on getting every molecule of oxygen into my bloodstream possible, and waiting for my opponent to come at me again. The guy thought he had the match won, and wanted to make it a big game of cat and mouse to finish up. Finally, the bastard came at me again, head down and moving in for the kill.

I waited. Waited. Last second.

And exploded to deliver a knee to the right ankle as I caught the guy and flipped him, hard, with an added bonus of using that foot for leverage and putting stress on the ankle.

The guy landed on his shoulder with a grunt and I didn't let up. Zeroing in on the right ankle, I hooked the foot for a minute to apply brutal pressure, then let the guy kick out. I followed with an axe kick as the spectators started getting excited.

And in moments it was over and my arm was raised as the winner. My opponent had to be helped from the ring by his handlers. I took my towel from Luke and stalked for the locker room. The girl, wearing a very bright red, curve-hugging dress and insanely high heels followed. Now what the hell was I going to do about that part of the prize?

I successfully delayed figuring it out for ten minutes while I got a shower and dressed again. Maybe she would just leave or whatever and I wouldn't have to deal with it. When Luke negotiated the prize package, I really hadn't believed him about the girl. I wanted the two grand, but I could get all the pussy I wanted without having to work for it. Luke finally convinced me though, and I signed on the line for the match.

I grabbed my stuff from the locker, shrugged into my Hell Raiders cut, and headed out, ready to get on with the evening. The damn cut on my cheekbone still oozed blood, and I brushed it away.

"Uh, hey, what should I do?" The girl tottered up beside me on the ridiculous heels.

I stopped long enough to take a good look at her. The fancy clothes didn't suit her, like I cared. She had the kind of curves that should be covered only by a bikini and some sexy ink. If I had time to play, she'd look great on the back of my Harley. Or on my cock.

I shrugged. "Do whatever you want. I don't care." Shaking my head, I shouldered through the door and out into the alley.

"Wait!" Her shoes clacked after me. "You won the night with me. So, uh…what do you want?"

I stopped and sighed, then turned to face her. "I know I won the night with you. I don't want it. So do whatever you want. To someone else."

Her face crumpled for an instant before she blinked and visibly pushed her hurt feelings aside. "I can't do that. Wherever you go tonight, I'm going."

What the hell? "Whatever. Doubt you'll like it much." I walked on toward the parking lot. Most of the spectators should still be inside, but I still paused at the corner to make sure no one was near my bike. Last thing I needed was some wanna-be tough guy trying to challenge me in the parking lot.

The woman followed, heels clicking along on the pavement, but I refused to shorten my stride to accommodate her. If she insisted on going along, she'd better keep the fuck up. I reached the bike and started to stow my gear in the saddlebag when she caught up.

"How am I supposed to go with you on that thing?"

"Not my problem."

One foot stamped in annoyance. "You're just about the rudest jerk on the planet."

"Rude? Me?" I paused to look up. "No, baby girl, I'm not rude. I'm saving you from yourself." Maybe that would get her to just leave me the hell alone.

"You are rude. If I don't go with you, Royse will add to my debt and it'll take two nights to repay him for this one."

I buckled the saddlebag and her words hit me in a delayed reaction. "Wait. What?"

She sighed. "I owe Royse money. If I don't want my mother living on the street with me, I have to pay him. He sets up the gig, I do it. But if I don't go through with one, I owe him two." A note of resignation crept into her voice. "Look, I get it.

You're gay, or whatever. Just let me tag along. I won't bother you. And in the morning when I call for pickup, you tell them I was great. Or even just grunt. I'll be a day closer to paying him of

A mix of emotion swirled over me, and I swallowed hard. The anger stayed put. "What?" I listened patiently while she explained in more detail. By the time she finished, the anger had multiplied. Everybody in town knew Royse as the go-to man for anything on the shady side, so little could be done about him taking advantage of women who would otherwise be homeless. I nodded and swung onto the bike. "Get on." She might have gotten herself into the mess with Royse, but I'd be damned if I'd make it worse for her.

Blank confusion settled over her face for a full minute before she bent to pull her shoes off. The dress presented a bit more trouble, but she finally settled for pulling the hem up around her hips. After a good bit of wriggling, she got the rest of it high enough to let her swing her leg over the fender.

I had to admit, she put on a pretty nice little show. One I could certainly appreciate. When she settled onto the seat behind me, I ran my right hand down her calf to grasp her ankle and guide her foot to the peg, then did the same on the left. Her warmth surrounded me as she leaned in and tried to hold onto her shoes and hold to my waist at the same time. The bike purred as I eased us out of the parking lot, then let it roar down the street.

At least I had the apartment to take her to. Normally, I would never consider taking a woman to my house, but the Hell Raiders would have just a little too much fun at my expense if I brought these particular winnings back to the club house. Besides, those sweet curves pressed up tight against my back made me doubt if I'd want to share.

The underground garage yawned ahead, the security lighting dim in the dark night. Damn thing reminded me of a monster, even though I parked the bike in the usual spot, and helped her climb off. Ironic that the feature that made the apartment most attractive—the secure parking area—also gave me nightmares.

The girl's hand felt tiny and unsure in mine as I led her to my apartment. Did she realize the sort of chance she took with her life? I wouldn't harm her, but the next john Royse set her up with could easily be a killer. Allowing a man to take her to his home, his turf, gave him free rein to do whatever he pleased, up to and including murder. The life of a whore was one big fucking game of Russian Roulette.

When I flipped the lights on, she stared with her mouth wide open. Whatever she might have expected of my home, apparently this was not it. She noticed the kitchen and gave it a closer look, her stomach rumbling loudly.

I dropped my keys onto the table just inside the door. "My name's Ryker, by the way. You hungry?"

"Elena. And yeah, if it's not too much trouble."

"No trouble. The bathroom's through there, if you want to freshen up while I fix something." I turned to the kitchen without another word, leaving her to fend for herself.

The Hell Raiders cut went to its customary place on a hook by the door and my shirt landed just inside the bedroom. Dinner sat a little higher on my list of priorities than a clean house at the moment. The gas range heated quickly and the steaks sizzled when I tossed them on.
With potatoes in the microwave, I turned to putting together a small salad.

I refused to consider what I was doing. Most of my Brothers had no idea where I lived. This place was a sanctuary, and I never shared it, never brought anyone home. Yet here I was, calmly preparing dinner for a woman I just met. Her hard luck story had obviously clouded my judgement.

Elena dropped her ridiculous shoes by the door and

alerted me to her presence. "Anything I can do to help?"

I turned to flash her a quick smile over my shoulder in my best attempt at being somewhat friendly and non-threatening. "How do you like your steak? And if you could grab plates and stuff, that'd be cool." How the fuck did people have others over? Just the thought of sharing my space with her, or anyone else, made me itch.

Blank confusion settled over her face for a minute. "Uh, I'm not picky."

"Medium okay then, just a little pink?"

"Yeah, that sounds good." She opened the cabinet I indicated and found plates for us, and silverware from the drawer.

"There's beer in the fridge, or there's water if you'd rather." I needed the beer to calm my damn nerves a little. Maybe then I would survive the meal.

She brought two bottles to the table while I put the steaks on plates, and added a mound of onions and mushrooms to each. Huge baked potatoes followed before I crossed to the fridge and grabbed the butter and two small bowls of salad. She seemed utterly amazed with the food, or maybe that look meant it wasn't good enough for her.

"Sorry, it's nothing fancy, but it should keep us from starving." I pulled a chair out and waited for her to sit, then dropped to my chair and twisted the top off my beer and took a long drink.

"It looks and smells amazing." The tip of the knife shook a little as she cut a bite from her steak and put it in her mouth. Her eyes closed and a low moan escaped her, going straight to my dick. "This might be the best thing I've ever tasted."

I smiled, more than a little relieved. This might not turn out so badly, after all. Last thing I needed was some high maintenance chick stuck in my apartment for the night. "I'm glad you like it." I took my first bite. "Can you tell me a little more about this deal you have with Royse? I didn't like the sound of it earlier."

She explained between bites and answered my questions, and didn't seem all that embarrassed about her part in the situation. By the time her plate was empty, she'd told me the whole sordid thing.

Anything I might say would come out nasty. so I just nodded and stood to take the plates to the sink. Shit like that, a man taking unfair advantage of people with no choice but to accept it, pissed me off. If she could turn to someone else, another pimp even, it wouldn't bother me so much. At least then she would have a choice. The anger buzzed along my nerve-endings again, but I tightened my shoulders to suppress it. Elena didn't need me poking into her business and making trouble for her.

Maybe a little too quick to stand, she almost lost her balance, but regained it quickly. "Here, let me take care of the dishes since you cooked."

Glad for a chance to let someone else do the dishes, I accepted and headed for the living room. Sprawled at one end of the big leather couch, I grabbed a paperback to keep my mind off the sexy little thing in the kitchen, and off her problems.

A surprised little sound escaped her when she came in from the kitchen and I glanced up. Dark eyes and lots of dark hair appealed to me, and she had that in spades, to go along with a hot little body. If she had a choice in the matter, temptation might overcome me. I refused to force myself on a woman, though, even if the force part came from someone else.

I dragged my gaze away from her. "It's early still. There's the remote if you want to watch TV, or if you're tired, you can have the bed and I'll crash here."

"What, are you really gay or something?" Those dark eyes went wide and she clapped her hand over her mouth. "I didn't mean...Not that gay is bad or anything, just—"

I raised a brow at her. She'd said that earlier too. If a male suggested anything similar, I'd have taken his head off. "I'm not gay. What gave you that idea?"

"Uh, well, most guys are all over free sex. I'm just a little surprised, I guess." She looked half sick with fear.

Her fright didn't set well with me, and I reached for whatever calmness possible to keep from scaring her more. I lifted a one shoulder in a half-shrug. "Well, I'm not most guys. Got a little self-control." The paperback landed on the coffee table with a light thud. "However, I'm not against the idea of sex with you. I'm against the idea of you being forced to do anything by some asshole, especially the way he's doing it." I wasn't opposed to the pussy business done right, if the girls were there because they chose to be, and they were safe and protected, besides earning good money. And certainly not ripped off like that.

Elena stood there, all those rocking little curves on display in that bright red dress, and her lips parted in something like surprise. She'd been so busy expecting me to jump her and arguing that I should, she didn't know what to think about what I said.

I patted the couch beside me. "Come sit with me."

She obeyed quickly, her slight weight barely denting the couch. My greater mass made her slide toward me, and I lifted my arm around her shoulders to pull her close. The pulse at the base of her throat fluttered wildly, betraying her apprehension.

She swallowed hard then turned a little and ran a finger down the center of my chest. "What would you like me to do?"

Ripples of awareness shot through me. "I don't want you to do anything you don't actually want to do. If you'd rather just crash for the night, I'm good with that. I can get all the pussy I want, without making a girl do anything she doesn't want to do."

"Thank you. I don't know what Royse expected, but he usually sets me up with jerks or nasty guys." She smiled a little, kind of shy. "For the first time in a long time, I was kind of looking forward to it."

Well hell. When she put it like that, how was I supposed refuse? My cock twitched with the thought of the things I'd like to do with her. "Well, okay then."

She leaned close and I dipped my head to taste her lips. Kissing normally wasn't my thing, but that mouth of hers definitely appealed to me. I kept it light at first but when she made a little sound of eagerness, I deepened the kiss. Her hands clenched on my shoulders, nails sinking into my skin. Damn she was a hot little thing. I needed space to explore all that, so I stood and scooped her up to head for the bedroom.

Still kissing her, I set her down, then backed off a little. "Let's get you outta that dress. That body shouldn't be covered up." I turned her around and pulled her hair aside to bare her neck for my mouth while I eased the zipper down and slipped the dress' straps off her shoulders.

The little moan she made when I swirled my tongue over the hollow of her collarbone prompted me to rake my teeth over the side of her neck. The moan turned into a sort of whimper that promised wet panties.

The tops of her tits looked neglected from my vantage point, so I slipped one hand around to her front to pay them some attention. Her nipples were already hard, and I rolled first one, then the other, between my thumb and finger, making her suck in a sharp breath.

My hard-on threatened to blow out my zipper, so I stepped back long enough to get my jeans opened and shoved partway down. She pushed her dress down over her hips to reveal a perfect little ass, which she immediately rocked back against me.

Fuck, I needed a condom. "Hold that thought, baby girl."

I rummaged in the bedside table for a moment and came up with one. Back behind her, I let my cock ride up between her ass cheeks, hissing at her heat.

She spread her legs and bent over, leaning across the bed. I needed no further invitation to drag the scrap of lace off her ass and sink one finger deep into her tight wet heat. She gasped and pushed back, seeking more.

I ripped the condom open with my teeth and rolled it on one-handed, then worked my finger out of her pussy to slide over her clit. My cock jerked with anticipation just before I drove into her with one smooth thrust. Fuck, she was tight.

"Rub your clit for me, baby girl." I slid my hands to her hips and guided her into rhythm as she complied.

The pitch of her cries indicated she was right at the edge. Rather than let her come immediately, I slowed my thrusts and went deeper, then withdrew entirely to turn her to her back. She immediately wrapped her legs around my hips and pulled me close.

I leaned over her and buried myself to the hilt and she clasped me even tighter. Over and over, I drove into her, until she gave a sharp cry and her pussy clenched. Before I knew it, my body had locked in orgasm as she drained me. I stood over her, heaving for air.

She smiled up at me. "Can we go again?"

I collapsed to the bed beside her, laughing. "Better let me catch my breath first."

Chapter One

Ryker:

The steam from the shower soothed my aching muscles and tender skin, and I stood there letting it do its work until I grew too tired to stay any longer. Bruised knuckles howled in protest as I grabbed the knob to stop the water.

The fight had been brutal and I would feel the effects for a few days. My opponent, though, would feel fucked up for weeks. The rep I gained in the underground fights brought me bigger and better opponents in the sanctioned fights. Tonight's legal fight made me work my ass off for the victory. That made the risk of being fined or banned for the illegal shit worth it. Nothing, not even the rules, were going to get in my way to the top.

The soft cotton towel felt more like sandpaper, but I persisted and dried myself thoroughly before putting on my favorite pajama pants, also cotton. Synthetic stuff wasn't healthy for the body or the environment, so I kept things as natural as I could without being gung-ho about it. Nobody knew that about me, though a few might have suspected.

In the kitchen, I grabbed a bowl and filled it with ice, then headed for the sofa. The TV came on to the twenty-four hour news channel I normally kept it on. Tonight, I needed it just for background noise for a few minutes, so I didn't bother finding something more interesting before I plunged both hands into the bowl of ice.

The shock made my breath hiss out between my teeth but I gained control quickly. Ice might feel like sticking my hands into a beehive at the moment, but my busted up hands needed it. So I resigned myself to twenty minutes of agony.

The damn news depressed me. More corrupt politicians insisted the government must cut whatever programs they deemed entitlements. Meanwhile, they raked it in hand over fist on the federal dime, and conspired against the only real chance our country had at digging out from the shit hole they put us in. All while Americans obsessed over which movie star fucked another's wife, and which model was too strung out to walk the runway.

Swallowing the urge to throw something at the screen, I dried one hand on my thigh and grabbed the remote to find something less idiotic. It wasn't easy. Sports were even worse than the news, with adults getting paid millions to play children's games. Finally, I settled on a reality show about living off the grid.

The prospect of living without electricity or modern conveniences piqued my imagination enough that the twenty minutes of ice torture passed relatively quickly. TV still on, I dumped the ice and turned to the problem of food. It wasn't a hard decision. Steak or chicken, broccoli or asparagus, kale or spinach, whole-grain rice or the twelve-grain bread I'd picked up yesterday. I settled on the chicken, asparagus, kale and bread, and quickly prepared it.

Most people thought I obsessed over food, but that wasn't the case. Sure, I liked food as much as the next guy, but it was a tool I needed to do my job well. Both of my jobs involved smashing faces, and I was very good at it. While I loved a big greasy pizza as much as the next red-blooded male, I almost always went for the foods that helped me do my jobs better.

Relaxing my usual routine a little, I grabbed a beer and took my plate to eat in front of the TV. Normally I drank water with meals, but after a fight, I always treated myself to a beer. And I almost never ate anywhere other than the table. Eating wasn't meant to be a passive activity and I didn't treat it as one. But this one time, fatigue pulled at my muscles hard enough that I kicked back on the couch to eat in front of the TV.

The show held my attention until it went off and another came on about people preparing for disaster or anarchy to strike. By the time that one went off, my mind had grown as tired as my muscles and demanded I head for bed.

My phone buzzed, signaling an incoming text, but I ignored it for the moment, cleaning up after myself instead. With everything back in its place, I finally checked.

K. Got work 4 u 2nite. S bringing details.

Well, hell. No reply required. And no questions tolerated. When Kellen and the Hell Raiders called, I was ready. Every fucking time. No exceptions. No matter what. Bed and rest would have to wait.

The intercom buzzed, two short bursts, letting me know Stella had arrived with the details. I buzzed the other Hell Raider in and unlocked the door, then grabbed my weapons to check them while I waited. The slide on the .45 came back easily, revealing an empty chamber, and I remedied that automatically as Stella let himself in.

I glanced up with a chin lift. "W'sup, Stella?"

The quiet biker closed the door behind him and locked it, then gave a wary glance around the apartment. "You alone?"

I grinned. "You know I don't bring anybody here, ever." Except two weeks ago, I did. Those words froze in my throat. None of my Brothers knew about the thing with Elena as a prize, and I sure as fuck had no intentions of telling them.

"People change." Stella lifted one shoulder in a half-assed shrug, but his probing stare stayed locked on my face. "And you didn't answer."

I shook my head. "I'm alone." The dude's fucking paranoia usually annoyed the piss out of me, but it served the Hell Raiders well. This time, though, I couldn't help feeling he knew something I'd rather he not.

His lazy grin seemed calculated to get under my skin, and it worked. But then he shrugged again and his face went serious, back to business. "Word is, some dickhead is trying to move in on Raider territory. Kellen wants us to look into it, all low-pro."

"Give me a minute." I stepped into the bedroom and dressed, not wasting time. Armed to the teeth, and then some, I headed back out. "Any idea who it is?"

"Nah, man, it ain't coming back to the usual suspects. But a truck load of electronics with a shipment of guns hidden in the crates disappeared into thin air. Then the guns magically appeared in the hands of some gang kids down in Louisville, associated with the Deuces." He paused to let that sink in.

Hell Raiders merchandise in possession of a street gang we'd long ago shut out meant somebody else had come into play in a very deliberate way. We were being set up. Fan-fucking-tastic. "What's the plan?" I already knew, but I had to ask anyway.

"Me and you's heading for Louisville tonight. Dig around and see what we find buried in the Deuces' back lot."

"A'ight. No rest for the wicked, I guess." I moved around him to grab my duffle out of the closet. "Ready when you are." The bag stayed packed and ready for just such a situation, though I stopped short of calling it a go-bag. That reminded me too much of a military, or law enforcement, operation. Not a good parallel for a man in my position to draw.

"By the way, man, since we're going low profile, cuts and Harleys stay put." Stella's announcement came as no surprise. We could hardly advertise our identities to this new rival and expect to learn anything. Besides, a Hell Raiders patch in Deuces territory served double duty as a target.

"No problem, but we're taking the Chevelle. I ain't riding in that heap you call a car." Two spaces came with the exorbitant rent I paid, and the black on black '70 Chevelle SS 454 I'd spent the past three years restoring sat in my other space. As much as I hated the prospect of putting her in danger, the old girl provided a far better ride than Stella's old Honda when it was brand new.

Stella gave another grin. "I was hoping you'd say that." No doubt he'd planned it out, and I'd fallen neatly for it.

The big block engine rumbled as I pulled her out of the space and waited for Stella to park his Harley. With our gear and weapons stowed in the back seat within easy reach, we rolled up the ramp to the exit. Less than fifteen minutes later, we were gassed up and ready to hit the road, and I gave one last regretful thought to my warm bed sitting empty. It would be a while before I had a chance to get a good rest. I fucking hated strange beds.

The only traffic on the narrow two-lane out of town was an old pickup with only one working headlight. Away from the lights and traffic of the small town, the rural road carved through the dark night. Unseen fields of corn, hay, and soybean spread to both sides, interrupted occasionally by a house or barn. I would have loved to let all four hundred and fifty horses in the big engine loose, but the dangers posed by deer leaping into the road restrained me. I hadn't spent all that time and money on the car to let some Bambi total her. So I kept my foot out of it, and kept the speed reasonable.

We finally made it to I-64, and after a quick pit-stop, we had a straight shot to Louisville and Deuces territory. "We have a plan when we hit town?" The question really wasn't necessary, but I hated going in totally blind.

"The Deuces have a fence that gets rid of whatever they pick up. We're going to him for some weapons, and hope he puts his new customers in touch with the source."

"Think it'll work? I could do without punching anybody this time. Hands fucking hurt after tonight's fight." The soreness in my knuckles had progressed from mild discomfort to a real distraction. I took my right hand off the wheel and worked it, trying to reduce the stiffness, then did the same with the left.

Stella shrugged. "Who knows. It has as good a chance of working as anything else."

He was right. Besides, it didn't really matter. We would adapt and work with whatever the situation gave us. That's what Hell Raiders did. A solid plan would make the OCD part of me more comfortable, for sure, but I had to admit, skirting along the edge kept me more alert. The Deuces were a nest of vipers, so alertness was a real asset in dealing with them.

Silence settled into the car once more, and I gave in to the temptation of open highway and no traffic. The engine responded eagerly, ready to test the limits. Adrenaline surged through my blood as the red needle hit one-ten and kept going. Just as I'd known she would, the Chevelle rose to the challenge and ate it up. Driving that car was a fucking rush I'd never get tired of.

I didn't let off until the signs warned of an approaching town. Headlights going East pricked the backs of my eyes, and I backed off the pedal. This time of night, cops were more likely to sit and wait for speeders near a town. A traffic stop would not go well, considering the weapons sitting on the backseat in easy reach. Neither of us had warrants, or even criminal records, in the names we currently used for official shit, but we'd learned long ago not to take unnecessary chances.

The needle hovered at the speed limit and I forced myself to be content with that. For the next two hours, we would pass smaller towns scattered along the highway every few miles. The risks far outweighed the thrill of speed, and the challenges of keeping the big car under control.

We neared Louisville, and Stella gave directions that took a less than direct route, and annoyance flashed over me. It meant I had to deal with downtown traffic in several towns along the way. The actual traffic should be sparse, considering the hour, but the maze of streets and alleys that always seemed to spring up out of nowhere got to me. Give me the highways and bypasses any time, if I couldn't have back roads and logging trails.

I managed it, though, and we rolled up into the edge of Louisville as the eastern sky started to lighten with the coming sunrise. The area had declined further in the several years since I'd been there. "Shit, we should have gotten a motel in Radcliff or something. I don't like the thought of parking my ride in front of any of these shit-holes."

"Don't worry, man, I got you covered. We got reservations."

Leary as hell, I followed his directions. Only to find myself at a three-hundred buck a night joint that made my jaw drop. Our check-in time might have raised an eyebrow, but when Stella paid for a week's stay, in cash, everything seemed just fine and dandy with the female clerk. Stella's outrageous flirting had nothing to do with her acceptance of us without question, of course. With everything taken care of, he palmed another two hundred and moved to shake the woman's hand. Her eyes flared wide with surprise when he pressed the bills into her fingers and gave her a wicked wink.

Huh. I wasn't quite sure what to think. This side of Stella, the biker with the Polish name nobody could pronounce, was entirely new to me. Bastard acted like he checked into fancy historic hotels every fucking day, and gave college girls a week's pay for a tip.

The questions waited, just barely, until I closed the fancy carved door behind us and paused to take in the room. I don't know what I expected, but this sure as hell wasn't it. A spacious bathroom caught my eye first, just to my left, and a big closet sat opposite it. Further in, a comfortable looking sofa and two chairs were arranged with a coffee table and a big armoire with one of the doors left open to reveal a TV inside. Beyond, a dining table with four chairs looked over a pretty little courtyard, and a desk filled the corner.

I walked into the room, wondering where the hell we were supposed to sleep. A door beyond the sitting area drew my attention, and I checked it out. Another room lay there, with two massive beds, a dresser, another closet, and another TV. All the fancy décor in the world meant absolutely nothing to me, but even I knew the rich fabrics were very good quality. While the outer room was mostly shades of gray and silver, with dark blue accents, the bedroom was a deep, rich blue with pale gray. That damned room cost more to decorate than my rent for a whole year.

While I stared at everything like a country bumpkin, Stella got busy. I hadn't noticed his bag earlier, but the sound of a zipper caught my attention. He opened a big garment bag, the kind rich guys carried fancy suits in, and lo and behold, the clothes he pulled out would be right at home in some rich business man's closet. He straightened creases and brushed away non-existent lint.

What the hell? I felt like I'd landed in an alternate universe. I cleared my throat. "So, how'd you get Kellen to come off the green to set this all up?"

"He didn't. This one's on me." Satisfied with the clothes, he grabbed a shaving kit and turned to the sink and mirror. "We won't get shit out of the Deuces if they realize who we are. So we're going back to my roots." A small cordless beard trimmer cleared away most of his facial hair, leaving a neat goatee.

"Roots?" I must have been as dumb as I felt. It wasn't unusual for Brothers to have a past they didn't bring to the Raiders. We were all running from something. But this seemed like an awfully fucking big something.

Stella sighed and dropped the trimmer, then turned

toward me, leaning one hip against the vanity counter. "Yeah. Roots. Ryker, brother, I need this shit to stay between us."

I nodded. "Absolutely." Seems like this might be a long story, and I was tired as fuck, so I dropped to sit on the fluffy sofa.

"You know my family is Eastern European—not actually Polish like I let everyone think. I won't get into all that. It gets complicated. But what you need to know is that my father came here after the Soviet Union fell. People were leaving the Eastern Bloc nations in droves, desperate for a new life. Among them, a few wolves left, eager to gain an advantage. That was my father."

I had a million questions, but I bit them back.

He continued. "He left behind an empire, one his father had built. His older brother stayed there to run things, and the whole family expected my father to fall on his face in the New World. But he didn't. He expanded and got his finger in every pie that connected the Old Country to the US. Drugs. Gambling. Prostitution. Weapons. Import-export. And a hundred other things. What he built makes the old empire look like a mom and pop shop at the corner."

He paused and lit a smoke, despite the clear No Smoking signs tucked discreetly all over the room. "I'm the oldest of four brothers, and all my life, I was groomed to take my father's place." Stella sighed. "I keep the connections, and sometimes help with business, but I can't be in the same room as my father, or I'll kill him."

The junk food I'd eaten on the road threatened to come back up. "Shit, man, I had no idea."

He shrugged and stubbed his cigarette out in a glass soap dish. "You weren't supposed to. Anyway, I'm here to put out feelers for distribution. You're my enforcer. We'll ask whatever questions we want, demand answers, and they won't dare think twice about it. I should have told you from the start we were coming in this way, but I had to make sure my father was on board and would back us up if anyone asked."

I sat back to think, not sure what to make of all this new information. At least now I understood why Stella was the go-to man whenever a job required ice water for blood. He'd grown up in a world that permitted absolutely no weakness or softness in a man.

"Does Kellen know any of this? Or how we're handling things here?"

"He ain't too happy about doing it this way. Thinks it's too risky. I've done this shit my whole life, though. It's the quickest way to get the info we want. Then we're out." He peeled his shirt off. "I'm going to get a shower, then start touching base with some connections here in town. We'll head out around three to see and be seen."

Relief settled into my tired muscles. "I'm going to hit the rack for a couple hours, then. Wake me a couple hours before we need to go out."

Stella nodded and gave me a half wave as he disappeared into the bathroom. I headed for the bedroom, and didn't bother to unpack my bag. My stuff didn't need hanging up, since wrinkles couldn't do it any harm, and the thought made me glad. A life of worrying about making a bad impression because of some lint didn't sound all that appealing to me. I could fall straight into bed and not worry about it.

I kicked my clothes off and slid under the sheets in just my boxers. The bed felt like a cloud, swallowing my tired muscles. Even if I did hate sleeping in a strange bed, this one was a close second to my own. I was out by the time my head settled into the perfect pillow.

Chapter Two

Elena:

For the ten millionth time in two weeks, my thoughts went to Ryker, and the night I spent with him. I'd never experienced anything like him in my life. Since him, Royse had set me up with every kind of jerk imaginable, and I had no clue why. At the moment I nursed a split lip and black eye to prove it. None of it made sense. Sure, I've had my share of bad dates, but they were usually pretty rare. Maybe my lucky streak had ended.

None of that mattered though. I fixed mom's lunch on the little two-burner stove in our one-room apartment. *That* was what mattered. I managed to keep a roof, even a shitty one, over our heads, and something like food in our bellies. The occasional split lip or black eye meant nothing next to those things. I steadfastly refused to let my brain go to the other parts of it. How many men I let stick their dicks in me, or how much I moaned and groaned for them, didn't matter either.

At least I wasn't doing it on the street. I knew several girls not lucky enough to have arrangements with Royse, and they had it far worse. No wonder they had to hit a little somethin' before they went out. Without protection, a working girl on the street turned into a living, breathing target for every sick fuck in the country. The right to say no to anything fell right out the window.

Mom made a sound that told me she was awake and in pain. "Morning, baby."

"Good morning, Mom. You ready to eat?" I poured the generic canned soup into a bowl for her and grabbed the crackers. Shit. She should be eating better than this. Fresh meats and vegetables, stuff like what Ryker made for me the other night. That might as well be gold and diamonds, though. Not like I'd ever afford either of them.

"You go ahead, baby. I'm just going to the bathroom. Still tired." She pushed off the bed with a groan that broke my heart and shuffled to our little bathroom.

When she came out, I was ready, taking her arm. "Come on, eat a little for me. You'll rest better." I led her toward the rickety table and helped her sit.

She took a reluctant bite. "You should be out having fun, baby, not sitting here with me."

The bright smile I gave her was fake as hell, but she wouldn't notice. She never did. "Don't worry, Mommy, I have plenty of fun. Now eat for me. I have to get ready for work soon and I won't be home until late." I made a mental note to check that she had snacks and drinks in the little box on the nightstand. Otherwise she wouldn't eat or drink the entire time I had to be gone.

She ate a few more bites while I made silly small-talk, then pushed back and said she was full. The smile she forced to her lips looked as fake as my own, and made her thin face look even more fragile. I gave her her meds, thanking God once more she'd qualified for free health care. I remembered all too well the days with no medication to ease her suffering.

With my mother all tucked in again, already sound asleep, I ate the rest of the soup rather than waste it, then started getting ready. The hot water had been broken for so long in our building I'd gotten used to icy showers, telling myself cold water was better for the skin. I'd picked that up on some stupid TV show at one time or another, I guess, but pretending the choice was mine made it a little easier to bear. In reality, I knew full well we were lucky to have running water at all.

Life hadn't always been so bleak. My father walked out

when I was really little, but Mom made it with hard work and determination. Back then, she worked in a factory making floor mats for cars, and we lived in a decent little apartment. It hadn't been *Lifestyles Of The Rich And Famous*, but it hadn't been bad either.

Then, my freshman year of high school, Mom got sick. I mean, really, *really* sick. She nearly died several times those first few weeks, running a high temperature they couldn't get under control, and had no idea what caused it. Her work was really good, gave her extra sick leave and everything.

But in the end, it didn't matter. The fevers let up, but that was about the only improvement. Now, almost ten years later, we still didn't know what caused it, or what kept her in constant pain. Maybe if we lived somewhere with fancy doctors, and could afford them, we might have found out. We had no other family, so I had to leave school to take care of her, and before long, that turned into trying to keep food and a roof, too.

Somehow, with sheer luck and the kindness of strangers, I kept it together for a few years, but it kept getting harder and harder. Finally, the eviction notices piled up and the landlord ran out of patience. He kicked us out, and because we had nowhere to go, we lost everything but what I could carry.

Partway through our first winter on the streets, I heard of a guy who could help with situations like ours, if he liked you well enough. I cleaned up in a convenience store bathroom, lied to Mom and left her at the library to stay warm, and went to see him.

Growing up like I did, with no time for boys, I was a virgin until the day I went to see Royse. He seemed to like me well enough. After he took the only thing I had left, he gave me money and told me to come back the next evening, he would have work for me. I've been a whore ever since.

Things could have been a lot worse, though, and I tried

to make the best of it. Until the night Royse set me up with Ryker, I thought I was doing a pretty good job of it. That night with him made me want more, though. I needed to find a way to get out from under Royse's thumb and do better for Mom and myself.

I had a cheap-ass cellphone Royse gave me so he could reach me when he wanted to, but I decided to use it for more. For the past week, I left the apartment early every afternoon in my one pair of decent jeans and a nice shirt I got for a nickel at the thrift store. Now, I had applications in all over town. If I could get something part time, I might be able to save enough to make a real start for Mom and me, and get away from Royse.

The one thing I had going for us was my GED. I'd studied every morning at the library until I managed to take that test and pass it. That piece of paper provided a ticket to the rest of the world. Or so I'd thought at the time. My ambitions had changed quite a bit since then. Now, instead of college and a big career, I would settle for a part time waitressing gig.

I checked on Mom one last time before I left, careful to lock up behind me. Our neighborhood wasn't one where you left anything to chance, ever. Heading down the stairs, I stayed quiet and paused on the landing before I reached the first floor. I listened carefully, but no sounds came from Juaquin's door.

Heart in my throat, I hurried on. I darted past the door in question, open as always. A hand snaked out and caught my arm, and no matter how hard I pulled, I couldn't break his grip.

"Why you wanna be like dat, mama? Come party wit' me." Juaquin dragged me against him and towered over me. "Got some real good shit."

I forced a smile and faced him. "No thanks, Juaquin. I gotta go, late for work."

He grinned, gold teeth flashing against his dark skin. "I done tol' you, mama, you don't need ta work. I be happy to take care of you and yo' sick mama, too. Make sure she don't hurt no more."

My heart pounded behind my eyeballs and I'm pretty sure he could see it. The man scared me pissless. He'd never threatened me, but Juaquin was the closest this neighborhood had to a drug kingpin, and he had a bloody rep. Refusing an offer from him was a quick way to piss him off. And still, if the need came up, I thought I could count on him for help in a bad situation.

I widened my smile and patted his hand. "Aw, that's sweet of you, Juaquin, it really is."

He let me pull away. "One o' these days, mama, you'll get sick of sucking dick for Royse. When you do, you just come to ol' Juaquin. Lady like you shouldn' hafta do that to keep her moms safe." He smiled, almost kind looking. "Don't forget, now, baby. You gots my number, call anytime." He released me and went back into his apartment.

I got the hell out of there and didn't slow down for a whole block. Less than a week ago, that man had one of his slingers come up short for the second time. He cut the guy's finger off. The whole area knew his brutal reputation and no one crossed him. So why the hell did he keep trying to be *nice* to me? He never asked a female twice if he decided he wanted her. They were all eager to get their hands on his drugs, and never said no. Yet I turned him down regularly, and he still offered to help me. I didn't get it.

Several other people gathered at the bus stop with me, waiting for a ride that never made it on time. Rather than make eye contact with any of them, I stayed firmly in my thoughts, trying to figure out Juaquin's game. My run-ins with him happened at least once a week, always with the same offer, and I always refused. And somehow, he hadn't slit my throat yet.

The bus finally showed up and I got on with everyone else. The dollar store on Second and a coffee shop down the street both had Help Wanted signs still in the windows, and I hurried to get my applications in.

The manager at the dollar store took my papers and looked me up and down, wearing an expression that promised she drank vinegar for breakfast every day. "Where you working now?"

My heart caught in my throat. "I do odd jobs when I can find them, cleaning and stuff like that."

Her look grew harder. "Never had a real job?"

"No, ma'am. I had to leave school to take care of my sick mother. I worked hard and got my GED, but I haven't been able to find a regular job yet." Some little scrap of pride urged me to just turn around and walk out, but I stayed put.

"Your mother still sick? You still taking care of her?"

Again, I wanted to run. "Yes, ma'am. But she doesn't need someone with her all the time now, so I can work." I took a shaky breath. "I'm a hard worker, ma'am, and I'm good with people. All I need is a chance." A silent prayer ran through my mind.

The woman smiled. "You be here at ten in the morning. I'll give you that chance."

Sudden tears burned my eyes. "You mean it?"

"Of course I do, honey. See you then."

"Thank you so much! I won't let you down." The tears rolled over. If only this woman knew how much her words meant to me, how they could change my life.

Happiness floated me down the street. Finally! Juggling work at the dollar store with nights for Royse might be tricky, but it should only take a couple of weeks. Once I got a pay check, I could get out from under his thumb.

While I made plans for how I would work and save to make things better for Mom and me, a big part of me trembled with fear. If Royse found out what I was doing, he would blow a gasket. He hated to lose. I had to make sure he didn't suspect.

I stopped off at the thrift store and bought two more

nickel shirts. They weren't anything fancy, but I couldn't show up to work in the same clothes every day, so they'd have to do. To celebrate my good fortune, I stopped and treated myself to a canned soda from the machine outside the little grocery store.

The cold, sugary goodness filled me with energy and I nearly skipped to the library, eager to share my good news with my one friend. Mrs. Carrington, the middle-aged lady that ran the little library knew my whole story. She'd been the one to encourage me when it seemed like getting my GED might never happen. Plenty of times, Mom and I wouldn't have eaten if not for Mrs. Carrington's kindness, even though she didn't have anything extra herself.

I pushed into the dim coolness and took a deep breath of books. That scent of paper and ink would always be tied to good things for me. Behind the counter, Mrs. Carrington looked up from the stack of books she was sorting, and gave me a broad smile.

"Good morning, Elena. My goodness, you look chipper today."

"You won't believe what just happened to me!" The long habit of dropping my voice to a near whisper when I came in those doors served me well and I managed not to scream out my news. "I got a job!"

Beaming, she came out from behind the counter and enveloped me in a hug. "Oh, Honey, tell me!"

I spilled it all, including my fears about Royse finding out and my earlier encounter with Juaquin.

"Honey, you deserve some good in your life. God will take care of making sure that man doesn't find out. Just let Him take care of it for you." Deeply religious, Mrs. Carrington practiced what she preached. She never considered herself better than anyone else, and she was kind to every single person lucky enough to come into her life. She knew exactly what I had to do, and she never once made me feel dirty or bad because of it.

I treasured her for the rare gift she was. "Today, I think I can actually believe that."

She smiled again. "Now all you need is for Him to put a nice young man in your path. Maybe that boxer, or someone like him."

I laughed. "Let's not get carried away. I'm completely satisfied if this job works out. I'm not greedy."

"Honey, you take my word for it. Every woman needs a man that can set her on fire like that, no matter how it starts out. You get a chance at him, you grab it with both hands." She gave me another hug. "Now, I've got some books to shelve. You need any help finding anything, you just let me know."

I thanked her and set off on my search, trying to decide what it would be this time. I might have missed out on high school, but thanks to Mrs. Carrington and the public library, I probably had a better education than I could have hoped for from the school system. I even knew which fork to use if I ever found myself at a fancy dinner, since I'd read one of the etiquette books.

Chapter Three

Ryker:

I stood with my back to the wall, trying to look as bored and disinterested as Tavis and Desmond's men. Stella finally managed to get a sit-down with the Deuces OGs. As an Enforcer, I don't usually get included in the power meetings and bullshit that goes on with the heads of MCs and other crews, and I was absolutely not interested. Politics bored the fuck out of me. But in my cover as Mr. Staladknovski's bodyguard, I didn't have much choice.

Rather than the mind-numbing exchange of nonsense and trash-talk I expected, I learned Stella knew how to get shit to the point. Even more interesting, he spoke with an Eastern European accent and no trace of his usual southern drawl. Everything about him was always redneck as hell, but suddenly my Brother seemed like he'd be equally comfortable at some high society gala. I couldn't wrap my head around it.

In a suit that probably cost more than I could make in a month of good fights, Stella sat straight and perfect in the cheap folding chair. "Gentlemen. I am here on behalf of the Staladknovski Family to inquire about certain goods our information indicates you have access to. If an amenable arrangement can be reached, we would be interested in acquiring these goods from your…organization."

Desmond, clearly in the bad gangster role, sat back and crossed his arms. His dark gaze missed nothing, especially not the Cartier watch with its alligator band. Hell, even I knew that thing cost more than a lot of houses. "What makes you so sure the Deuces want to make any kind of arrangement with you or your family?"

"You would like to wear a watch worth more than one hundred thousand dollars, yes? Five thousand dollar shoes? A twenty thousand dollar suit?" He waited for a flicker of greed in Desmond's eyes. "I see, you would. Then you see how a business arrangement with my family could be profitable, I'm sure."

Desmond shrugged and stared for a moment. "Why the Deuces? You got that much green, you can get any fucking body to sell you what you want."

"You are new, and hungry. You will work harder than an established enterprise to meet our needs."

Desmond exchanged a look with Tavis, who shrugged. "What you got in mind, man?"

Stella's shoulders tightened, just the faintest bit, and instantly put me on alert. "I am in the market for certain types of hardware. Which I am told you have access to."

Tavis scowled and I suddenly readjusted my assessment of who the bad gangster was in this pair. "Look, homes, I ain't tryna jack you or nothin'. But quit beatin' aroun' the motherfuckin' bush and say it straight out, or I bounce."

Stella stayed silent for a long moment. "Fine. My people tell me you have access to guns in the quantities I need."

"Guns, huh? When my boys tol' me you was askin' around, I checked you out."

"And what did you find?" The tension in Stella's shoulders increased, and I sensed the explosion that would come if he got the wrong reply.

"You keep your word and you get what you want. And nobody sees you. So why you here instead o' having' somebody else do the legwork?" Tavis dropped the gangster talk.

The sharp bastard suspected a setup. I shifted a little to make sure my knife could hit him in the throat if the need arose. If this shit went sideways, I was taking him out first.

No need to worry though. "I was in town for other business. This," Stella made a gesture as if to include the whole area, that fancy watch glittering and catching the light, "is just a side project."

Tavis looked to Desmond and they seemed to communicate without words, then Desmond spoke again. "I don't know, man. We could probably work somethin' out."

Tavis slapped a hand on the table. "What the fuck? You know we'd have to get with Royse first." He rose from his seat. "Fuck this. I'm out. Ain't making no deal." With his bodyguard in the lead, Tavis slouched from the room, slamming the door on his way.

Desmond raised his hands and let them drop. "Well, that's it. Thanks, but we can't do it."

Stella dropped his head in feigned remorse. The loss of the deal meant nothing, now that we knew who the supplier was.

I knew Royse all too well. Keeping my face blank through Stella closing the meeting was harder than I'd thought it might be. Everything I knew about the low-life kept churning through my head, and I really needed to talk it through with Stella, but it would have to wait.

The three minutes until we walked out went down in the record books for the longest stretch of one hundred and eighty seconds ever. Out on the street, we climbed into the rental Stella insisted on for this little leg of the mission, and got the hell back to our hotel.

We hit our room in total agreement. Stella changed back to himself, and I packed our shit at double speed. The faster we got out of Louisville, the happier I would be. And I'd rather not have a Deuces bullet in my head when I hit the city limits.

One good thing about traipsing around town for the better part of a week, I'd found several alternative routes out of town and acquainted myself with the back alleys and short cuts.

As soon as we checked out, I had the Chevelle fired up and ready. We'd kept the car under wraps during our stay, so hopefully Tavis and Desmond would think we were driving the nice luxury sedan we rented.

I turned toward the rear exit of the parking garage, ready to make our escape. The time in Louisville wore on my nerves, and I itched for action of some kind, even just the chance the drive fast. Fucking pitiful.

"Where you going, man?" Stella leaned to look over his shoulder and check oncoming traffic for me.

Pride inflated my chest, just a little. "I found us some different routes out of town, while I was out for my runs in the mornings. Ol' Tavis and Desmond will think we're still sitting in the hotel."

Stella grinned. "Good thinking. Especially since I had a couple porters head out in the rental. They'll head over to the airport and drop it off for us, after they roll around town a while and run out some gas. By the time the Deuces' boys get a look at who's in it, we'll be halfway home."

Once, as we wound our way through narrow down-town streets working our way toward one of the many small towns Louisville had swallowed during its growth, I thought I spotted a tail in the rearview. Stella watched, though, and the suspicious car dropped away, and nothing took its place. We both breathed a lot easier by the time we hit Elizabethtown and the Bluegrass Parkway carried us toward home.

Stags Leap hadn't changed a single particle during our absence. Of course, I hadn't expected it to. Damn place *never* changed. Well, with the exception of the ATM on the corner across from the Rattlesnake. Even the gas station still used the old analog pumps. All two of them. Reminded me every time I went there of why I moved across the river. Small towns had their advantages, but for someone that wanted to move up on the MMA circuit, the drawbacks outweighed them.

Several Hell Raiders' bikes sat at the Rattlesnake, so I turned into the gravel lot so we could find out where Kellen was hiding out. We had to track the bastard down and let him know what we'd found out in Louisville.

The parking lot lights made the paint gleam over the Chevelle's hood. Damn, it would take me a fucking week to get all the dead bugs and dirt off. I gave the car a silent apology and headed inside with Stella.

Rita's Rattlesnake Tavern had an odd layout, and the owner converted it from family diner to bar every evening, with a live band and all. We made our way through the entry and headed for the bar and a cold beer. The band rocked their version of Guns 'N Roses *Welcome To The Jungle* to a packed house.

And in the middle of the crowd, the Hell Raiders' usual table sat like an island. The regulars knew not to get too close, even without the glares from Fabio and some of the other Raiders. We weren't always welcome in the Rattlesnake, but that shit got sorted a while back.

Beer in hand, I made my way over and dropped into a chair. A chin lift to Fabio took care of the helloes. "Kellen been around?"

Badger, the head of the Raiders Home Guard, leaned back in his seat. "Nah, man, he's out at the clubhouse. He best be careful, though. Staying this late, his ol' lady might lock him out of the house." Everyone around the table laughed, even though we all knew it wouldn't happen. Vicki, Kellen's woman, had her own business to run, so she understood.

We sat there and exchanged gossip and finished our beers, then headed back out. Shit, I really hated the idea of taking the Chevelle up that damn dirt lane to the clubhouse, but it couldn't be helped. I slowed way down for the turn to make sure I missed the hellacious pothole Kellen kept not getting fixed.

Stella laughed. "What the fuck, man? It's already dirty. You have to wash it, what's a little more dirt?"

"See, fucker, that's why you drive a beat to hell Toyota. I don't need gravel pings or chips. And dirt's an abrasive. Enough of it will eat a paint job over time." Bastard. Should know better than give me grief over the car. Kellen's pickup sat in a grassy area to one side, and I pulled in beside it.

One of the guys from the Rattlesnake called ahead and Kellen met us on the porch. After the usual arm clasp greeting, we followed him to his office. Stella summed up our trip quickly, and we waited for Kellen's questions.

"They had no idea you were Raiders?"

The laugh wouldn't stay put. "Nah, man, you should see Stella all cleaned up. Looks like a regular rich dude. And we left everything Hell Raider back at my place so there wouldn't be a chance of someone seeing."

"Good." He asked a few more questions about specific details, and we answered. "Ryker, you know Royse, right?"

"As little as possible. He's a slimy bastard. Organizes some of the underground fights, loan shark, bookmaking, pimps out chicks who owe him." That thing with Elena still pissed me off. Hell, if it hadn't been for our grandparents helping, back when my mom got sick, that could have been my fucking sister. I was just a kid at the time, but my older sister got a job to help out until mom was back on her feet. But what if our grandparents hadn't been there? Or if mom hadn't recovered?

Kellen nodded. "Does he know you're a Hell Raider?"

"I doubt it. He doesn't pay any attention to the fighters beyond setting odds and making money off us."

"Good. Okay, let me think about this for a bit. Need to get you into his inner circle so we can bring his ass down hard." He sort of waved us away. "Go on, get out of here, get some rest. I'll call you when I have something."

Stella stayed quiet as we drove out of Stags Leap and

headed across the river. It was a safe bet he wanted his secret kept safe, but he wouldn't disrespect me by asking. Well, he had nothing to worry about. Other than busting his chops a little about cleaning up like a rich dude, I wouldn't say anything.

Chapter Four

Elena:

Fuck. It was a bad date, my third in a week, but this one took it to a new level when his fist smashed into my face. An open-handed slap, or even a backhand, was one thing, but a fist could do serious damage. A couple of bruises, or a cut lip, could be covered up. Swelling and gashes couldn't.

Suspicion hit when Royse sent me to motel I hadn't been to before. He normally used one of three, and the staff knew us, and I think some of them even sort of looked out for us. A new motel meant absolutely no safety net. And I suddenly needed one.

The john drew back to hit again, and I braced myself. Sure, I could have probably ducked or something, but that tended to just piss them off more and make the beating worse. Better to take a couple of hits than to get myself shot. That was one of the first lessons I learned about hooking. The blow rocked my head back and my vision went dark for a few seconds. Panic hit hard and made me try to pull away before he could hit me again.

Big mistake.

"Get back here, you stupid cunt! I did not say you could move." Heavy alcohol fumes from his breath burned my eyes. The next punch made me cry out, and he stifled it with a hand over my mouth. "You make another sound and I'll kill you."

This one wasn't going to stop with a few bruises and a split lip. I forced my muscles to go soft. I had to do whatever it took to stay alive until I could get away. He hit me again and I didn't need to fake my knees going weak. I sagged in his grip and fought to breathe through the pain.

He thrust me away from him and I stumbled and fell to the floor against the flimsy stand that held the TV. The stand banged into the wall and sagged, and I had to roll out of the way as the TV crashed to the floor. For just an instant, he froze and fear flashed in his eyes.

Something heavy banged against the wall from the other side. "Keep it down in there, or I'm calling the cops!" The male voice from the next room sounded seriously pissed.

"Sorry, dropped something," my date called out in reply.

I drew a breath to scream in the same instant a huge knife appeared in his hand. He made a threatening gesture, warning me to stay quiet.

He fully intended to kill me. I saw it clear as day in his face.

I let that scream loose and scrambled back, grabbing the broken leg of the TV stand as I went. Muffled curses from the next room reached my ears, letting me know I'd been heard. I screamed again, holding that damn piece of splintered wood in front of me like it could stop him.

"Hold on! I'm calling nine-one-one!" The shout came through the wall loud and clear.

My date pointed the knife at me and glared. "You fucking bitch. I will get you for this." And then he was gone. Just like that. Gone.

The faint echo of sirens came to me through the open door. I took a deep breath and said a little prayer of thanks. That came way too close.

The shakes started as the sirens came closer. I stumbled to the bed and sat, sort of hugging myself, and just tried to keep it together.

Realization hit. Oh. My. Fucking. God. Royse had set me up. I was supposed to die.

He *knew*!

Somehow, he found out my plans. This was his way of making sure I didn't get out.

Tears rolled down my face to mix with the blood from my split lip, and probably plenty of mascara, too, but I didn't care. What could I do? If he kept sending me to men he'd told to hurt me, or kill me, I wouldn't last long.

Two fucking weeks. I needed two more weeks before my first paycheck from the store. I wracked my brain for another way to get the money for mom and me to live on until then. The only answers I came up with were worse than Royse. What the fuck was I going to do?

I sat there and waited. No sense running at this point. My blood was all over the room, so they wouldn't have to try very hard to track me down, and then I'd have even more questions to answer. All too soon, the blue lights lit up the parking lot outside, strobing off the walls of the room.

The first cop came in with his gun drawn. "Who else is here?"

"Nobody now. He left." My voice sounded weird.

He still checked everywhere, including the moldy bathroom, while his partner waited just outside the door. Finally, he holstered his gun and came to stand in front of me. "We have the paramedics on the way, miss. Can you tell me what happened here?"

I went through it, leaving out certain details, like my being there as a whore. No need to catch a solicitation charge.

The cop looked doubtful, but the paramedics came in and sort of occupied me, so I couldn't easily answer questions. They kept saying I should go to the hospital and get checked for a concussion. That idea made me laugh. Like I could afford that shit. Finally, after a couple of butterfly strips and an ice pack, they made me sign that I refused transport.

By the time they let me leave, I itched to just crawl under the covers and hide from the world for a week. Too bad.

If I did that, Royse would take my covers, along with everything else I'd managed to squirrel away.

My phone buzzed while I waited at the bus stop. I glanced at the screen. "Hi Royse, you calling to see if that bastard managed to kill me for you?" Anger mixed with the tiredness that already shook my bones until they hurt.

He took a deep breath, and I could easily imagine him looking upward, as if his life were so difficult. "What are you talking about, Elena?"

I glanced around. The young guy at the other end of the bench could have been a student, I guess, but it didn't matter. I'd rather not advertise what I was. Bad enough Royse did that. "This was the third bad job you've sent me on this week. And this one nearly killed me. Just lucky for me, he heard sirens and left." He couldn't know the guy in the next room called the cops, or that I made enough noise to raise suspicions.

He stayed silent for a minute, probably making notes about what to ask the john. Or how to find somebody who could do the job right. "Are you okay? Did he mark you up?"

A laugh that didn't sound at all like me came from my throat. "Of course not. Unless you count the black eye, the gash on my cheek, or the busted lip. Pretty sure there's a few other marks, too. Did you think he would kill me and leave a perfect corpse?"

The student guy glanced sideways at me and stood, moving outside the little shelter. Who could blame him? He probably thought whoever beat the hell out of me would come back for me, and didn't intend to be there for it.

"Elena." Royse's tone sent a shiver down my spine. "I don't like what you're implying. Go home, sleep it off, and come see me at the office tomorrow morning." He hung up, the threat hanging clear in my ear.

I put my phone back in my purse and slumped back on the bench to wait another half hour for the bus. Being broke sucked. I wanted nothing more than a hot shower and the lumpy bed I shared with my mom, but here I was stuck on a hard bench as the night air started to chill.

The shower at the motel had been tempting, but that guy still had the key card. With my luck, he'd come back in and catch me. Better to make do with the cold shower at home. I should have told Royse to send one of the drivers to pick me up. He set this up, the least he could do was make sure I had a ride back home.

A car drove past, really slow, and the driver sure seemed to pay a lot of attention to the bus stop, but finally, it went on. A bright orange scooter buzzed around the corner and down the street.

The bus eventually rolled up, and I stood, aching all over, and climbed on. The driver went out of his way to hit every pothole he could find and every jolt shot pain through my bones. The four stops before mine seemed like a hundred, but I survived, and when the time came, stepped off the bus just two blocks from home.

At times like this, it was hard not to notice how seedy the area was. Right by the bus stop, three boarded up businesses stood as reminders. Layer upon layer of graffiti covered their brick walls, and cigarette butts and broken glass had piled up against the edges of the sidewalk.

I tried to walk a little faster past the alley that yawned between two of the buildings. The place always gave me the creeps, bad. The stupid heels Royse always made me wear clicked on the concrete, and told any damn fool a woman walked down the street.

Something clattered a few feet back in the alley and my heart jumped into my throat. It took everything I had not to run, even though I knew it would let anyone watching know how scared I was. A woman showing fear, on the street alone, at night might as well just stand still and let them get her. So I concentrated on walking, staying alert, and getting my ass home.

Movement caught my eye in the vacant lot across the street, and I nearly stopped in my tracks. Three bangers made their way through the high grass, staring straight at me. Fear turned my legs to jelly and they refused to cooperate.

One of the men brandished a gun in my direction. "Get on out of here, bitch. Ain't got time to pop a cap in your head."

He didn't have to tell me twice. I ran.

The heels didn't make it easy, but I managed.

Halfway through the next block, I stumbled and my ankle rolled painfully. A few steps further, the heel broke off the same shoe. I kept going.

Despite the odds, I made it to my building, out of breath and holding my side. Dread shot through me as I pushed through the door and into the stairwell. Hopefully, Juaquin wouldn't hear me and come out asking questions. I should have known better than to hope, though.

"Elena?" He came out, and hissed when he saw my face in the crappy light. "What the hell happened to you?" His fingers were gentle as he pushed my hair back to get a better look.

"It's nothing." I drew back from his touch. "I have to get up to mom."

"Girl, you go in looking like that, she's gonna flip her shit. You need to clean up first."

I started to shake my head, but it hurt too much. "Not much of a way to clean this shit up. A black eye I can handle, but there's swelling, too."

His eyes narrowed. "You ain't see yourself, have you? You got a hella lot more than a black eye to fix up." He caught my elbow in a soft grip. "Come inside. You need to get the blood off your face, at least. You look like you been in a zombie fight or some shit."

As bad as I hated to go into his apartment, when he put it like that, I had to protect mom. When something upset her, she hurt worse. "Okay." I followed him through his door.

The muted TV made weird shadows on everything, but I made out a couch, and a coffee table with a laptop computer open on it. As he directed me through a door to the bathroom, I suddenly realized Juaquin's apartment was twice the size of the others. He actually had a separate bedroom, with a door and everything.

His bathroom was bigger, too, with an actual bathtub instead of just a crappy shower stall. The harsh light burned my eyes, especially since it was right over the mirror. The face staring back at me belonged to a stranger. My cheek was swollen and dark purple. The white of the butterfly strip stood out stark against my skin. The eye on the same side was swollen almost closed, the visible white part filled with blood.

Makeup had run all over my face, and mixed with blood. The dried mixture really did make me look like I'd come through a war zone or something. Juaquin was right. If mom saw that, she'd have lost her shit.

Chapter Five

Ryker:

I fell into bed, exhausted. I had to be in the gym around six to get warmed up. Less than three days to prepare for my next fight, and I had to make the most of every minute. Juggling training with work sucked, but when Hell Raiders business got thrown into the mix, I came out on the losing side of all of it.

For the time being, I had no choice, though. Fighting paid most of my expenses, but I wanted a safety cushion. I've thought of asking Kellen to back off what I'm asked to do for the Raiders, but can't bring myself to do it. Those bastards have had my back for so long, I would feel like shit if I let anything slide with them. No, I just had to figure it out and try my best to keep it in balance.

Despite my being worn out, sleep took its time coming. No doubt, I owed that to Elena. The next fight was one of Royse's, and I couldn't help but wonder if she would be part of the prize again. That thought led to a raging hard-on that refused to just go away. Thoughts of Elena helped my hand take care of the situation, and my damn brain finally shut down for the night.

The fucking alarmed dragged me out of bed at five thirty, and even though I felt like I'd only just closed my eyes, I got up. I pulled on a T-shirt and workout shorts, grabbed my bag and headed out the door. Out on the street, I slung the bag over my shoulder, stretched, and took off in a jog. The six-block run would wake me up and get my muscles firing just in time to get started on training.

The city was quiet this time of morning, and I always

enjoyed my little run to sort of get my thoughts in order for the day. Not many people were out and about so early, so I normally had the street to myself. Today, though, I spotted another runner up ahead. Curious to see if it was somebody I knew, I stretched my strides a little and started closing the distance.

Within a hundred feet, I nearly stumbled when I realized the other runner was female. In the six years since I moved here to be closer to the gym, I made this exact same run at least three times a week. In all that time, I've never once encountered a female runner.

Dark shorts hinted at the curve of a shapely ass, and long, toned legs practically hypnotized me. I quickened my pace to pull closer for a better look. Dark hair pulled into a braid lay forward over her shoulder.

Before long, I came close enough to see how her sweat-dampened shirt clung to her skin. I must have spooked her, because about a block before the gym, she cut over to the other side of the street. Oh well. I had more important shit to take care of, anyway. I stretched out and ran hard the last hundred yards, and hit the gym door panting and wiping sweat.

Luke spotted me from where he had a couple of newbies warming up. I lifted a hand and stashed my bag, and started straight into my warmup routine. Luke would catch up with me for footwork and technique training, but until then, my day would follow the program. Too bad I didn't have the day off work, so I could devote the entire day to training and resting.

After three hours of working hard, Luke waved me to the showers. I had just enough time to swing back by my apartment and grab my lunch before I had to be at work. Hopefully it would be a light day and I could rest a little. Of course, every time I hoped for that, we'd get slammed.

The next days passed in a blur of training, work, and more training. No problem getting to sleep at night with a schedule like that. I didn't have to work the day of the fight, so I spent the time with light training and re-watching videos of my opponent for the bout. Royse had four matches slated for the night, and mine was the Main Event.

I made a quick stop at the gym for a last minute strategy talk with Luke, then climbed back on my Harley for the ride to the next town. Royse held his fights in an old factory, closed years ago and boarded up. No one questioned a couple hundred vehicles sitting outside an abandoned building on a Saturday night. No doubt, they knew better. Royse's goons had a rep for liking blood.

I parked at the corner of the lot, like always, and headed in the side entrance. Some of the factory's old offices had been converted to locker rooms, and rather than wait for Luke to arrive, I staked out space in the largest one. As a head-liner, any place I wanted to get dressed was mine. Law of the jungle, baby.

The crowd of spectators roared to signal the end of the first match. I changed and spent some time warming up and going over takedowns in my head. Luke arrived in time to help me finish up, and spent every spare second reminding me of my opponent's weaknesses. He didn't tell me, but I knew Royse was giving the other guy good odds to win. Good thing that had never stopped me before.

Royse had tried to get me to throw one of my early fights for him, but I made clear if he wanted me in his cage, I didn't throw a damn thing. He backed down, but whenever he put heavy odds on the other guy, I knew it would be a hard fight.

Somebody stuck his head in the door for my five-minute warning. I never liked waiting until the last minute, so Luke and I headed out. Something about the energy of the crowd always amped me up, and this time was no different. The place was packed and they were all excited about the Main Event. My pulse raced in reaction and I took a second to focus on breathing.

With the big spotlights focused on the cage, the spectators weren't easy to see, but I still looked, just like always. Just off to my right, a flash of red caught my eye, and I turned to look fully. It was stupid, really. Even if Elena was there, she'd had on a different dress. Except she was, and she didn't. The same bright red dress clung to every delicious curve, and the memory of taking it off her flashed through my head to make my mouth water.

Elena looked anything but happy to be with the big man who kept a possessive arm around her shoulder, while Royse looked as thrilled as a kid with his first girly magazine. That look on Royse's face set off all kinds of alarm bells in my head, but I didn't have time to wonder why. Especially when my attention kept going back to Elena. It seemed she was going to be a regular part of the entertainment for the underground fights, then. I tried to ignore the flare of jealousy the thought brought.

The third match ended and the announcer waited for the crowd to quiet a little, then called the fighters for the Main Event. From there, everything blurred together until the bell for the opening round. Then, just like always, I focused in tight on my opponent. I already knew how he liked to fight from the videos. What I didn't know yet was whether he'd stubbed his toe getting out of bed, or if he'd taken things a little too hard in training. So I watched and anticipated.

We both advanced quickly into a cautious exchange to test each other, searching for weaknesses. A female scream, way too close to the wire, snapped my attention away from the match. The other guy saw and took advantage, closing fast with a flurry of kicks and punches.

I had to scramble, but I managed to block most of it and still strike back. A good kick put him off balance and when he retreated, I followed hard.

At the end of the round, I backed off. "What the fuck was that, man?" Luke's anger came through loud and clear. I shook my head and shrugged. "Well, you make sure it don't happen again, you hear me?" I nodded, and at the bell, went back out.

Wary now, my opponent tried to keep some distance, but I pursued for a takedown. I let him kick out, fully aware it took more energy from him than me. After another exchange of kicks and punches, the round ended.

Until the third round, I minimized the use of my knees, keeping them in reserve. Then I used them to systematically pound the other guy until he reeled at the end of the round. In the fourth, I allowed him a brief rally to get the spectators going again, then made my own comeback just before the bell.

Seconds before the bell for the fifth, my focus took another dangerous shift to a flash of movement just beyond the cage. A slim form in red struggled against someone much larger. Elena. Anger rolled through me and I wished the fucker man-handling her stood in the cage tonight so I could take him apart.

Enough fucking around. At the bell, I went out hard and dismantled the other guy until he collapsed. I barely managed to wait for my arm to be raised for the decisive win before I bolted from the cage.

The spectators roared, cheering the win, congratulating each other if they'd bet on me, and pissed if they didn't. Somewhere in all that mess, Elena needed help. Even though I knew it was a stupid move on my part, I needed to get to her. The damn crowd surged, either eager to get out ahead of the traffic, or collect their winnings, or both.

The damn lights came up, blinding me and showing the spectators the way out. Unable to spot her in that clusterfuck, I headed for Royse's usual seats. He would be there until he'd either collected or paid on all the bets of the night. I figured he would have to pay out quite a bit, since the fight didn't go his way.

It took a few minutes to wade through the crowd, but I finally spotted Royse, right where I figured he'd be. One of his goons leaned in to whisper to him, and Royse looked in my direction as his mouth tightened. Not surprisingly, he seemed more than a little pissed at me.

Nobody had the balls to contest my right to be there as I shouldered people out of the way and approached. They were lucky they didn't, or I might have taken some heads off. It suited my mood perfectly to take some of the goons apart.

"Ryker." Royse's growl said he wasn't happy to see me. "You cost me a lot of money tonight."

I took a second to restrain myself. "Too bad, man. Smart money was on me." My fists stayed ready at my sides, just in case. The bastard had been known to have fighters jumped for less.

He scowled. "Luke will have your winnings when I wrap up here. Hit the showers. You reek."

I grinned, though it probably looked more like a snarl. "I'm sure I do. Luke will get with you. I'm here for something else."

"Yeah? What would that be?" He counted out another man's winnings and scowled in my direction.

"Earlier, before the match, I saw somebody I thought I knew. Don't see him now and wondered where he'd got to. He was with you and that hot little *chica* from the last match. Big guy. Know who I mean?" As bad as I wanted to demand he tell me Elena's whereabouts, I couldn't give him that kind of power. Even though my interest amounted to nothing more than curiosity, he would assume it was more and try to use her against me.

Royse narrowed his gaze at someone slightly beyond me

and gave his head a little shake. On instinct, I whirled, expecting to catch someone trying to jump me from behind.

Instead, the big man drew near, dragging a protesting Elena with him. Even in the low light, the thin line of blood at the corner of her mouth was plain as day. Fuck.

Rage shot through me, and I had to consciously lock my muscles to keep from doing anything to get myself killed.

Hope crossed Elena's face. "Ryker! Help me, please!"

Shit, if I made the wrong move... I shook my head and turned back to Royse. "Nah, not who I thought it was." I shrugged and made as if to move on past.

One of Royse's goons moved out of my way just a bit too slow, and I grabbed him, swinging him between me and the others while I snatched the .45 from his hideaway holster.

"What the fuck, Ryker?" Royse started to stand.

"Move, Royse, and I'll blow that gold tooth down your fucking throat." A quick lift of my chin indicated the big man. "You tell him to let her go. Now. Unless you and the rest of these nice people want to see how good a shot I am."

Royse nodded at the other man, and Elena pulled away from him and ran past me. "This is a big mistake, Ryker. I'll ruin you for this shit."

I grinned at him. "Nah, you won't do that. I'm your cash bull these days. You think I don't know about the money that changes hands here? I ain't blind, fucker. You need me." Giving the goon a hard shove that took down his two colleagues, I beat it for my locker room.

They would need at most five minutes before they came to take me apart, so I had no time to waste. To my surprise, Elena waited for me just inside the door. With no time for explanations, I grabbed my bag and her arm and got the hell out of there.

"Ditch those fucking shoes and come on."

She followed orders surprisingly well for a female, and

by the time we reached my bike, she already had her dress up and ready to climb on. I kept my bag over my shoulder, just in case I needed the .45 inside, and started the Harley. She held on tight as I got us the fuck out of there.

Chapter Six

Elena:

Why did I even ask him for help? Sure, no other john has had the least bit of concern for me, and Ryker helped me the first time by letting me go with him. But this time, I knew it would put him in danger, and I still asked.

And he ignored me. My heart stopped when he seemed to not even see me there with the Russian. In that moment, I had no doubt, I wouldn't see the morning.

And when the chance came, when Ryker chose to rescue me? I sure as fuck didn't turn it down. After my last date, I knew nothing but a miracle could save me and my mom. That night when I got home, she hadn't been there. Royse had taken her and left nothing but a note telling me she was safe as long as I played nice. Apparently, playing nice meant letting my date kill me.

A shiver ran through me despite the warmth of the night. I guess I'd stopped playing nice. As far as I knew, they'd killed her already, but if they hadn't, Royse would give the order after what happened at the fights. Either way, I was no good to her dead.

For the moment, all I could do was concentrate on staying behind Ryker and hoping I lived through the night ahead. In the morning, I would have to find some kind of answer.

Not even ten minutes from the factory, Ryker slowed his bike and pulled off the road. I raised my cheek off his back to look around, my heart pounding with fear. Or had I jumped from the frying pan into the fire? After all, I really knew nothing about Ryker, except he was amazing in bed. Or had Royse's men caught up so soon?

But no, there was nothing around. No lights. No traffic. No buildings. Just empty countryside stretched away in the dim moonlight. A new chill chased itself down my spine as I realized exactly how small and vulnerable I was in the middle of all this nothing.

Ryker shut the bike off. "Okay, climb off real quick. I need to get dressed in case we hit trouble." His words made me feel foolish for being afraid of him. Wearing nothing but the shorts he wore for the fight, of course he needed clothes.

As soon as I was off the bike, he climbed off and stripped out of his shorts. "What happened back there? Who was that guy?" He pulled clothes out of his bag and started putting them on.

I shook my head. "I only know him as the Russian. He's one of Royse's mob connections, I think. What little I know about him, or Royse, for that matter, comes from the other girls. Sometimes we actually get a chance to talk."

"Tell me."

"Girls that leave the fights with the Russian are never seen again. Royse owes him, or at least, fears him. He didn't even put up a fight when the Russian wanted his niece, even though she wasn't part of the line-up. Just handed her over with a smile. She never came back, either." I didn't know what else to tell him, so I waited and shivered.

He dragged his shirt over his head. "Okay. Hold that thought." He dug around in one of the bags on the back of his bike and made a satisfied noise as he held up a cellphone about like mine. "Knew I kept that bitch in there for a reason." He powered the phone up, and as bad as I wanted to ask what he was doing, I held it while he punched in a number. "Hey, man, it's me. Got a little situation. Meet me at the trestle in thirty?"

Without waiting for a reply, he turned the phone off and

pulled it apart. The battery went back in his bag, while the phone itself hit the pavement to be crushed under his heavy boot. His gaze raked over me, missing nothing. Looking thoughtful, he fished in the bag on the other side, and pulled out a flannel shirt.

"Put this on. I can't do anything about your legs right now, but maybe that'll help a little." He tossed the shirt my way. "We have a fifteen-minute ride ahead, and part of it will be a little rough. Nothing I can do about that either. When we get there, I'll have to take a little walk and talk to my buddy. You stay at the bike and don't move. Understood?"

I nodded and buttoned the shirt, grateful for it. He got back on the bike, and I waited for him get it started and gesture for me to climb behind him. Wherever he intended to take me must be even more in the middle of nowhere. No other cars came into sight from either direction.

At one point, I caught the sparkle of moonlight on a lot of water. Once more, I felt fear at Ryker's intentions, but I tried to shake it off. Surely he wouldn't have gone to the trouble of rescuing me from the Russian just to kill me himself? He put himself in serious danger from both Royse, and the Russian. I doubted he would go to that much trouble just to turn around and kill me himself.

He slowed and turned off the road onto a gravel track. When he hit the first bump, I felt it all the way up my spine. The second came not even a heartbeat later. I quickly lost track of everything except trying to hold on and keep all my teeth in my mouth.

The path came to a sudden end in a tiny clearing and he stopped the bike. I climbed off when he told me to.

"Remember what I said, Elena. Do not leave this spot under any circumstances. I'll be back in a few minutes. Understand?"

I nodded.

He took my shoulders in a firm grip. "I need the words, Elena."

"I understand. I'll stay here."

"Good girl." He handed me the bag he'd brought his clothes in from the fights. "If you're hungry or thirsty, there's water and a protein bar in the side pocket. I'll be back soon."

And just like that, he disappeared from sight. The sound of his footsteps reached me for a couple more minutes, but then that was gone, too.

Fear made my mouth painfully dry, so I searched his bag for the water he'd mentioned. After a few swallows, I took a careful look around. The darkness hid things I'd rather not think about, but I could make out the path that brought us to the middle of nowhere.

A long time later, Ryker still hadn't returned, and I tried to decide what to do. Surely he didn't mean me to stay there forever? What if something had happened to him? I couldn't just sit there and hope for another rescuer. I made my way to the edge of the path, but quickly turned back when the sharp rocks cut into my bare feet.

Discouraged and scared, I went back to the bike and dropped to sit beside it. The damp grass chilled my legs, but I stayed put. If he never came back, I would die there, anyway. What difference did it make if I caught a cold?

Tired as fuck from the stress of the last few days, I put his bag beside me and lay down, using it for a pillow. At the moment, just curling up to die seemed like as good a choice as any. I must have dozed off, because the next thing I knew, a warm hand stroked over my cheek.

"Come on, Elena, time to rise and shine."

There for just a second, I thought the whole damn mess might have been a bad dream. But then I moved a little and a rock dug painfully into the side of my thigh.

"That's my girl. Come on, got you some clothes." He

helped me stand with gentle hands, and didn't let go until I'd stretched and steadied myself. "Here, put these on. They're not much, but better than that dress."

I nodded and shoved my legs into blessedly dry, warm jeans. They were too big, but it didn't matter, they felt fantastic. He handed me a pair of sneakers and turned to do something at the back of his bike. I put the shoes on and managed to tie them tightly enough they might not fall off my feet.

"Here. I don't have an extra belt, but this should help with the pants." I held my dress and shirt up while he bent to fiddle with something at my waist. "There. That should do it." He stepped back. "Why don't you ditch that dress and I'll find you a hat?"

It grew a little lighter with every passing minute, and the trees all around were full of chirping birds. Morning.

I pulled the dress off and happily dropped it to the ground, then put his shirt back on, and took the baseball cap he offered.

"Pull your hair through the back of it. That'll help keep it out of both our faces on the road." He got on the bike while I followed orders. "Ready for breakfast?"

My stomach answered for me with a loud growl.

He grinned. "I'll take that as a yes. Come on, let's go."

I climbed on and held on tight as he took us back over the bumpy trail, which I saw had once been a railroad. They'd removed the rails and the ties, leaving the rock base with deep gouges where the ties had once been.

Thankfully, that ended, and in ten minutes or so, he pulled into a fast food place and parked. I climbed off as soon as he stopped the bike, not at all steady. In the near full light, he took a long look at me, then looped his arm around my waist and led me toward the door.

"The ladies room is just inside the door. You'll want to stop in there first. I'll wait for you, and we'll go on inside together. Understood?"

Memory flashed back to the last time he issued orders, and I spoke instead of just nodding. "I understand."

"Good girl." He pulled me tight to his side for a moment, then opened the door for me.

In the restroom, I got a glimpse of my face in the mirror as I rushed for the toilet. Damn, no wonder he wanted me to go there first. I'd be ashamed to be seen with me, too. I flushed and went to inspect the damage.

I couldn't do much about the fresh bruise on my jaw, or the fading one on my cheek. Wet paper towels took care of the dirt that caked the side of my face, and the blood dried over my lip and chin. With no hope of getting rid of all the heavy makeup, I used a damp paper towel to try and even it out a little. I even managed to blend a little over the bruises. Satisfied I'd done all I could, I went back out to find Ryker right where he promised he would wait.

He nodded approvingly. "You clean up pretty good, Elena." With his arm around me once more, he held the inner door open and guided me to the counter. "Get whatever you'd like."

The prices were fucking ridiculous. Even though I felt like I could eat two of everything on the menu, I forced my eyes to the dollar section. "Um, just hash browns and coffee, please."

Ryker gave me an odd look for an instant. "She'll have the pancake breakfast, too, with bacon, and scrambled eggs. I'll have the same, and coffee. Add two large OJs, too."

I squirmed uncomfortably while he paid and accepted our tray, then followed him to a table. The coffee smelled delicious and I took a careful sip as soon as he handed it to me.

He put our food on the table and dropped the tray on the neighboring table. "One rule, Elena."

My heart thundered at the sternness of his voice. I waited, too scared to ask.

"While you're with me, you eat. Understood?"

"I-I understand."

He winked at me. "Good girl. Now dig in. We have a long day ahead of us."

Chapter Seven

Ryker:

Elena ate like she'd never seen breakfast food before. That, combined with the memory of her eating the steak that night at my place, made me think she probably didn't eat too regularly. Her story must be a harsh one. Those bruises on her face said life hadn't been too nice recently.

"Tell me a little more about yourself, Elena." Of course, I only asked to make conversation, not through any real curiosity.

She shrugged a little. "There really isn't that much to tell."

It was going to be like that, huh? "Why don't you start by telling me how you became involved with Royse in the first place?"

She pushed the food around on her plate a little. "It isn't a pretty story, Ryker. I'd rather not go back through it all."

"I get that." I paused, trying to think of a gentle way to get her to tell me. Since I'd taken her from him, her problems were now mine. "Look, if I'm going to help you get out of that, I need to know a little. Don't worry about details. Just the general facts."

Dark eyes filled with tears, but she blinked them away with determination. "Okay, don't say I didn't warn you." She went on to tell me about her mother getting sick, about surviving on the kindness of strangers, and then Royse. "That was my last resort. I looked for work, everywhere. But no one hires a seventeen-year-old high school dropout. The shelters here only take in men. They'd have to have better space and stuff for women and kids, and they just don't. So, I did what I had to do. And I'm still doing it."

As she spoke, my heart broke a little for her. My earlier thought about how my sister could have ended up in a similar situation was right on the mark. "Now tell me about those bruises."

"I was going to get out of the life. Make a new start. I found a real job, at a store, but I had to keep working for him for another two weeks, until I got my first paycheck." She paused and shook her head. "I don't know how, but he must have found out. He sent me on three bad dates in the last week, and the last one was going to kill me. Then last night."

I stayed quiet and ate a little. Definitely not what I was supposed to have, but these were extreme circumstances. "Okay, here's what's going to happen. You're going to disappear. You'll stay at my place until we make other arrangements."

A stubborn tilt of her head served as my only warning. "I can't. Royse has my mom. If I don't go back, he'll have her killed. If he hasn't already."

Well shit. That put a new monkey wrench in the works. By now, Stella would have passed on what I told him at the trestle, and Kellen would have taken other steps to stop Royse's interference with Raiders business. Most likely violent steps. Which would put Elena's mother in even greater danger.

"If you're finished eating, we'll go back to my place, and I'll call some friends and have them find your mom."

She grabbed the tray from the next table and started piling our trash on it. "Let's go."

As we rode, I tried to think more than one step ahead. Royse would have men looking for us both, at least until I made things clear to him, so we had to stay out of sight. I needed to get in touch with Luke and tell him to lay low for a while, too, just in case they decided to go after him in order to get to me.

The parking garage had a rarely used, and mostly unknown, rear access, and I chose to go in that way, just in case Royse had someone watching my place. The tight alley leading to that entrance presented no problems with my bike, but for a car it would have been nearly impossible.

We made it upstairs and I paused to arm the alarm system I'd installed as an added precaution. The building's security would keep out, or at least slow down, most people, but I didn't know what kind of skills Royse's men had. No need to take unnecessary chances.

A hot shower sounded great, but I couldn't yet. Too much shit to take care of. Elena would probably like one, though. "If you'd like a shower, I can probably find a T-shirt and some drawstring shorts for you. Doubt I have anything else that wouldn't fall off of you."

"I need to be doing something to find my mom." The worry on her face struck a chord in me.

The need to reassure her and offer comfort came from nowhere, blindsiding me. "Let me work on that for now. You won't be any good to her when we find her if you're hurting and exhausted." I led her to the bathroom. "Get started, I'll find those clothes for you."

She nodded and went to follow orders, while I started the search for something for her to wear. Memory of the last time she'd been in my apartment tugged at my cock, and the temptation to not find the clothes failed to surprise me. I wouldn't mind if she just stayed naked, but she probably would. I sighed and dug out a T-shirt I hoped wouldn't entirely swallow her, and a pair of long shorts with a drawstring at the waist.

Temptation hit hard when I stopped to leave the clothes in the bathroom for her. She'd already started the water, and the pebbled glass of the shower doors offered a tantalizing hint of naked body.

"Leaving these with the towels for you, Elena." I dropped the shirt and shorts and beat a hasty retreat. In the kitchen, I grabbed a protein shake, hoping to undo a little of the damage from breakfast, the headed for the couch to start making calls.

A vague pounding started in the back of my head. Looked like I'd gotten myself into a real mess this time. Just another day. I dialed Kellen first, and updated him myself.

To say my president was unhappy was like comparing a pissed off tiger with a sore tooth to a fluffy house cat. "What the fuck were you thinking, Ryker? Some stray piece of tail can't interfere with business. You know that shit."

Ever since I rolled out of the parking lot of that abandoned factory, sweaty from the fight and still way underdressed, with Elena on the back of my bike, I'd been thinking of what to say when Kellen asked. "I know, man. I followed my gut, and maybe I should have found another way. But there's something up with Royse, something bigger."

Kellen grunted. "What do you mean, something bigger? What the fuck is bigger than stepping in Raiders business?"

"I think he's fronting for somebody." There. I'd said it.

"Who? And why?"

"There's always at least one of a couple different dudes at the fights with him. Kinda hanging back, but a presence, you know what I mean? The fucker there last night, I've seen him a bunch of times. He was dragging the girl around, had hit her a couple times already. She said they call him the Russian. And he's a VIP, gets his pick of Royse's girls, even though those girls never come back. And that made me think of Vicki's Russians." I knew in my bones that man had his hand in Royse's business, one way or another. If he had connections to the Russian mob, they could possibly be the same crew Kellen's old lady ran up against when they first met.

"A'ight, Ryker. We'll get somebody else inside.

Meantime, you make that bitch disappear, and get your shit together. You're the only one we have that can get close, and you're already inside. Make peace and get your ass back in there."

"That somebody else that gets inside, I need him to look for something."

"What's that?"

I explained about Elena's mother and held my breath. He could easily tell me to forget that shit.

"Okay. I'll see what can be done." He hung up, having said all he intended to on the matter.

I took a deep breath and busted the burner phone. For the next call, I used my regular phone. "Yo, Luke." The line went dead. Guess he was pissed. I dialed again.

"Why the hell you callin' me, you little bastard?" Yeah. Pissed.

"Guess Royse told you, huh?"

"Yeah, he tol' me alright. While a couple of his boys pounded on my head."

"Shit. Man, I'm sorry, Luke." Guilt sucker punched me in the gut. Luke was a good guy. He didn't deserve that shit.

He sighed. "I just hope she's worth it, Ryker. You burnt some big bridges."

I thought about that for a second. Maybe I was wrong about Royse putting money from my fights above revenge. Was she worth it? "You think I could talk to Royse? Apologize, or some shit?"

A pained laugh echoed in my ear. "Sure, man, you could do that. If you want your hands busted. Ryker, you didn't just grab some whore from a spectator. You took the bitch a big backer wanted. And you made Royse look like he didn't have his shit under wraps. Made him lose face."

I ran a hand through my hair as that sunk in. "Fuck."

"Yeah. Fuck." Ice rattled in a glass on his end. "Look,

kid, best thing you can do is disappear. No more underground fights. Even if another organizer would touch you after that, any time your name comes up on the circuit, he's going to be gunnin' for you. And he won't stop at anything to break you."

"Well, man, that don't work for me. I have to make peace with Royse and get back in the cage."

"Didn't you hear a fucking word I just said, kid? What, you got a death wish or something?"

I took a gamble. "I heard you, Luke. But I've got other business with him. And to take care of that, I have to be there."

"Shit."

"Yeah."

"Okay. Lay low for now. I'll try to smooth things a little for you to make a sincere apology." I could imagine him shaking his head at the thought. "Give me a couple days. I'll get back to you."

"A'ight. Thanks, Luke. Means a lot, man." I hung up and pocketed my phone, then collapsed back on the couch. Telling Luke I had other business with Royse was a big risk. Even though I hadn't told him the nature of what I had to take care of, he could still choose to rat my ass out.

Elena came in. "Thank you. I feel almost human again." She stood there, her damp hair in loose waves around her shoulders, my shirt concealing her curves, and the marks of violence on her pretty face.

I forced my thoughts away from what her body looked like under my clothes. Something about her wearing my stuff made things shift around in my brain. It had hit a little last night when she pulled on the shirt from my bag, but this was different.

"Good." I patted the couch beside me. "Have a seat."

She complied, not in the least hesitant. A scent I recognized as uniquely hers surrounded me, mingled with the smell of soap and shampoo.

"I hope you like TV, or books. We're going to stay out of sight here for a couple of days. I contacted somebody about finding you mom."

Big tears filled her dark eyes before she could blink them away. "You did?"

"Yeah. Not sure how long it'll take to dig in, but it's underway."

The tears spilled over. "Thank you. I didn't think you actually meant it."

A knot of foreign emotion tightened in my belly. I brushed her tears away with my thumb. "Of course I meant it."

She sort of collapsed against me, and I just sat there, unsure what to do. Finally, I put my arms around her and held her close while she sobbed into my chest. What did I know about comforting an upset woman? Absolutely nothing. All I could do was let her cry and hold her.

Chapter Eight

Elena:

Part of me didn't care that I looked like a complete idiot to Ryker. The other part hoped like hell I didn't leave a ton of snot all over his shirt. No matter how embarrassed I was, I still couldn't make it stop. It seemed like the stress of the last few days, worry about my mom, and the fear, all decided to come out at once.

And through it all, he held me close and stroked my hair, even though I had the feeling he wasn't sure what to do. It worked, anyway. Gradually, I managed to bring my tears under control, or I ran out. Either way, it slowed to sort of shuddering dry sobs.

"Better?" The low rumble of his voice caught me off guard and I pulled away a little.

I nodded and covered my face with my hands. "I'm sorry. I didn't mean to…"

"Shh, nothing to be sorry for. You've had a rough time." He smoothed a warm hand down my back.

"Yeah, but… Excuse me, I must look terrible." I lunged to my feet and ran for the safety of the bathroom. What the hell brought that on? I *never* cried, not since that first night when I went to work for Royse. And most especially not in front of anybody. I felt like a fool. Ryker probably thought I was one of those women that turned on the waterworks to get her way, when nothing could be farther from the truth.

A deep shaky breath later, I finally looked at myself in his mirror. My eyes were red, swollen nearly shut, and red blotches stood out on my skin. The bruises I collected over the last few days stood out like new ones. My head hurt like I'd been on a three-day bender.

I soaked a fluffy washcloth in cold water and held it to my face, hoping to ease some of the swelling, at least. Finally, I looked a little better and gathered my courage to go back out and face Ryker.

He sat on the couch, where I'd left him, but his shirt lay on the coffee table. When I came in, he looked up with a careful smile. "You okay?"

What could I say? "I think so. Look, I'm really sorry for falling to pieces like that. It's not something I do." My face burned with shame.

He stood and held out one hand toward me. "Come here."

I followed orders, and sat beside him when he pulled me down.

"Elena, I'm not all that smart. Hell, I let dangerous fighters pound on me for a living. But I do know a couple of things." A gentle finger tipped my chin, forcing me to meet his gaze. "I know when a person has been through serious stress, especially over a long time, there's a breaking point. It will only stay bottled up for so long. I also know that now you've let some of it out, you'll be able to deal a little better."

The kindness in his gray eyes threatened to overwhelm me again. No one had ever treated me this way, like I mattered. Well, nobody but my mom, and she hadn't been able to in a while.

He seemed to recognize my rapid blinking for what it was, and smiled for a moment, then lifted me into his lap. "Stop worrying, Elena. I got you."

I gave in and let myself collapse against his smooth chest, and just let him hold me. We sat that way for a long time, and gradually, memory of the texture of his skin under my lips forced its way into my mind. Ryker was the only man I'd ever been with who bothered to care that I enjoyed sex, too. And there he was, half naked, warm skin next to my lips again.

I knew I shouldn't. He was kind enough to get me out of whatever hell Royse had planned for me, and he'd said he would help find my mom. In spite of that, and maybe a little because of it, I couldn't resist. My lips brushed lightly against him, just a tiny bit. Maybe he wouldn't even notice.

Wrong. His hand came to the back of my head to press me closer. And I didn't resist. Instead, my mouth parted for my tongue to taste his salty-sweet skin. A groan rumbled through him, just before he gripped my hair and tugged my head back.

Ryker's mouth descended on mine, possessing, taking. His kiss was unlike anything I'd ever experienced, a mixture of sweet and hard. I let myself get lost in it, in him, let him take away all the bad in the world.

His fingers tugged at the hem of my shirt, and I leaned back a little to give him access. Warmth brushed against my stomach as he lifted the shirt and his fingers trailed up my ribs to find my breast. He lay me back against the couch and deepened his kiss until we were both forced to break away for air.

I barely noticed as he slid the shirt off over my head, until his mouth returned to mine, his chest warm against my bare skin. His kiss made me want so much more, both from him, and from life. In his arms, I could dare to dream of the happily ever after that never came to girls like me.

He brushed a thumb across my nipple and I arched against him, until his lips left mine and scattered little kisses down my neck. He paused at the curve of my shoulder, teasing the sensitive skin and sending shockwaves through my body. How had I never known I liked being touched that way?

Simple. Nobody had ever taken the time to do it, and now that Ryker was, every nerve ending I owned seemed determined to make up for lost time. When he finally reached my nipple, he teased, swirling his tongue until I ached, and then going to the other.

I dug my nails into his shoulders, begging for more, but he refused to give more than his own maddening pace. Sleek skin over hard muscle called to my hands to explore, and I did just that, skimming my fingertips over his arms and back up to his chest. I found his nipple and paused there, brushing my nail over the pebbled skin, to see if it affected him as strongly as it did me.

Ryker rolled his head back with a growl and a curse. "Who the fuck makes couches so damn small?" He stood and scooped me up in one movement, and stalked for his bedroom.

My pulse pounded, caught between fear and anticipation. He sat me on the bed, right in the middle, as if I were the most precious thing on earth. For a second, he stood there, just looking at me. Finding fault, seeing all the ugly parts. Instinct raised my hands, trying to cover myself, before he could turn away in disgust.

"No. Don't hide from me, Elena." He sat on the bed at my side and pulled my hands back. "You are the most beautiful woman I've ever seen. Don't take that from me." He leaned in, his breath warm against my cheek, and then his lips found mine again.

I'd seen movies, fairy tales, where the world tilted and fireworks went off when the hero kissed the girl, but I knew those were bullshit. In my world, nothing like that happened. If the girl was lucky, the hero didn't beat the piss out of her when he got what he wanted. Except with Ryker, the world *did* kind of tilt, and I could have sworn I heard fireworks going off all around us.

He kissed down my body, lingering at my breasts again and making me want something that didn't exist, before continuing further. When his lips met the waist of my shorts, I thought he might stop, but instead, he worked the drawstring loose, and took forever sliding them down my hips.

I shook like a junkie needing her next fix when he drew my knees apart and settled his shoulders between them. He hadn't done that before. No one had. Something told me I would never be the same afterward.

That mixture of fear and anticipation returned full force, with a healthy dose of shame mixed in. What if I smelled awful or tasted worse?

Ryker didn't seem to have any doubts, though. He licked and kissed, searching out, and finding, every secret, until I forgot to worry. My entire body responded to every flick, every hum, until I felt like I would fall apart if he didn't do something else.

And then he did. He slid a finger inside me, rough calluses against flesh gone insanely sensitive.

And I did fall apart. Right there under his mouth. Heat flashed over me and my muscles locked down, refusing to let him go. He stayed right there with me, until I had to push him away because it was too much, too good.

If I thought he was finished, the gleam in his eyes would have told me otherwise as he stood and shoved his jeans down. His hard length hypnotized me as he rounded the bed and bent to search in the nightstand.

To my surprise, he lay on the bed at my side and held out a condom still in the wrapper. "Put it on for me?"

When I sat up, he shifted to his back and closer to the middle of the bed. I looked at the condom packet, then at him, and smiled as an idea took form in my mind. I rose onto my knees at his side, then bent forward to kiss him. Tasting myself on his lips came as a bit of a shock, but I liked it.

I let my fingers slide over his warm skin, exploring the contours of muscle and bone. Ryker was such a strange mix of hard and soft, rough and smooth. I could spend years learning his body, and still not know everything I wanted to. When I reached his cock, it was like the rest of him, silky soft skin over hard heat. I took my time to place the condom and roll it down, enjoying the way his muscles quivered under my touch.

"You're killing me, here, Elena." In a flash, he grabbed my hips and rolled me under him. "My turn, baby girl."

He slid into me with one sleek thrust, and for the second time, my world tilted a little.

Chapter Nine

Ryker:

I drove my cock into Elena's body and got lost. That's the only way I could explain it. Nothing existed, beyond driving her sweet body to orgasm again, and burying myself in her until I reached my own.

I liked sex as much as, or more than, the next guy, and I had plenty of it. But I always stayed at least a little aware of what went on around me. With Elena, I didn't bother to know anything beyond how sweet her cries sounded, or how tightly her body gripped me. Nothing else mattered.

When her muscles locked around me, I forgot any other woman had ever existed. Even while I came into her, I knew it would never be enough. No matter the cost, I needed her again. I would pay any price, up to and including my life, just to have her.

I collapsed a little to one side and focused on catching my breath and my sanity. What the fuck? I wasn't the type to believe in true love or any of that other romance movie bullshit. That shit didn't happen in real life. No, in reality, a lucky guy found a chick he could tolerate more than ten minutes at a stretch, and maybe had a kid with her, then spent the rest of his life regretting the one time he left the rubber off.

Well, not me. I would never be *that* guy.

Sure, I'd promised to help her find her mom, and I would. But then it was over. She went back to her life, I went back to mine. Period. All I had to do was keep us both alive until then. That might be easier said than done.

***

I woke up to the late-afternoon sun slanting in through my bedroom window. Elena's head still lay on my chest, and her hair tickled my jaw. She looked innocent in sleep, and soft. I'd fallen asleep with her curled against my side and her arm across my chest, but she'd moved. She'd reached up, her palm against my face, as if she wanted to remember it forever, and her thigh lay across my hips, pulling me even closer.

What the hell had I been thinking? I'd asked myself that question a few thousand times since I ran out of the abandoned factory with her. And I still came up with the same damn answer. She needed me. What kind of fucked up was that? Some chick needed me, I just put the whole damn world on hold? I refused to admit Elena might not be just some chick. My life didn't work that way.

She stirred a little at my side, as if my thoughts woke her. "Hey." She smiled up at me, with all the possibilities of the world in her eyes.

"Hey, you." I tightened my arm around her. "Rest okay?"

She laughed a little. "I don't think I've ever slept like that."

"What, naked beside a man who just worshipped your body?"

"That, too." A giggle bubbled up, and I suddenly realized I would do many things to hear that sound again.

Fuck, I was an idiot. "You hungry?"

She nodded. "Yeah, I am."

"Good. I'm going to cook for you." I sat up as she moved. "After I get a quick shower. God, why didn't you tell me I reeked? I just realized I didn't even clean up after the fight."

She looked up at me through dark lashes and lifted one shoulder. "I like it. You smell… honest."

That one threw me for a loop. "Honest?"

She shrugged. "Honest. Other men, they cover up their

scent, try to make it all flowery or spicy. Just like they cover up the truth. I've had enough lies to last a lifetime. I like honest."

Okay, then. I grinned. "Well, you might like the truth, but I don't think I can survive this stench for long." I leaned down and kissed her, surprising myself. Kissing outside sex wasn't my thing. "Five minutes, baby girl."

I probably broke some kind of record getting clean, and I didn't go easy on the deodorant, even if Elena did say she liked honest. I hadn't thought to bring anything to wear into the bathroom, so I headed back for my room to grab something. Elena stood at the foot of my bed, wearing my shorts and pulling my shirt over her head.

Seeing her there like that, in the middle of all that was mine, made me wonder things I shouldn't. I grinned at her. "Told you, five minutes."

Another of those addicting giggles of hers. "So I see. You're a man of your word, just like I thought."

Yeah, that shit was a drug. I *needed* to hear that laugh again. A lot. I grabbed a pair of clean shorts and pulled them on. "That I am." I stepped close and pulled her into my arms. "And I seem to remember some words about feeding you. Still hungry?"

Her head came just below my shoulder, so she stood on tiptoe to meet my kiss while she laughed again. "Starved."

"Hmmm. Good to know." Yeah, playing house with Elena for a couple of days could prove very dangerous to my sanity, if nothing else. I released her and headed for the kitchen. If I didn't find a way to gain some distance, I was pretty sure I could drown in her.

The kitchen held mostly foods for a fighter in training, and even if I wasn't as fanatic about it as some guys, this mission to find chick-food might have set me up for failure. A trip to the grocery store waited in my fairly near future, I figured.

Even so, I found some chicken breasts, brown rice, and broccoli. Might be able to turn that into something real people might eat.

"What can I do to help?" Elena leaned one hip against the counter and watched me get things out. "I can't cook, so it'll have to be fool proof." She gave a nervous little laugh.

The insecurity bothered me. A woman like Elena should never doubt herself. And there I was, right at the edge of the danger of spending time with her. I couldn't get too attached, and even though I was the kind of guy who rarely fucked the same woman twice, I could feel it. I was already too attached. Fuck.

"Want to chop the broccoli?" I directed her to the cutting board and knives, and told her how I wanted it cut.

The meal came out pretty good. Elena seemed impressed. At least, she didn't throw it at me. I wasn't used to cooking for, or eating with, anyone else, so how much I wanted her to like it came as a bit of a surprise.

Watching her eat turned into a form of torture, though. Every bite she took, she closed her eyes, chewed slowly, and made this little moan-purr of appreciation. My dick twitched with every single bite and my imagination ran wild. A trip to the store was definitely in order.

When she finished, Elena sat back, eyes sparkling. "That was really good. Thank you."

"I'm glad you liked it. I was worried there for a minute. I'm not used to cooking for anybody else."

She stood and started clearing the table. "You cooked, so I'll clean up."

I sat mesmerized and watched as she carried the dishes to the sink and started washing up. It might have crossed my mind to get up and help her, but then I caught a glimpse of the curve of her ass in my shorts, and I froze. All I could think of was how that smooth skin had felt under my hands earlier, and how much I wanted to see and touch again.

She turned and caught me staring at her, and I didn't look away. She gave a little smile, like she knew exactly what I wanted to do. The movement of her body held my undivided attention as she wiped down counters, then came to wipe the table.

By the time she finished, I couldn't take it anymore. I caught her arm and pulled her into my lap. Her little squeal of surprise made me want more, and I threaded my fingers through her hair to guide her head down for my kiss. I licked her lower lip, slow and deliberate, enjoying her taste, before I pushed into her mouth to explore the tender perfection.

My phone buzzed in the living room, where I'd left it on the coffee table, but I ignored it and let it go to voicemail. Nothing felt more important than possessing Elena again. She gave a little moan and relaxed into my arms.

The phone started up again, warning me that whoever was calling intended to speak to me. "Hold that thought, baby girl." I gently set her back on her feet and went to catch the call. "What?"

"I'll be at your door in about three minutes. Buzz me up quick, yeah?" Stella hung up without waiting for my reply. Rude bastard.

Elena came out from the kitchen as I dropped the phone back on the coffee table. "Everything okay?"

I shrugged. "Not sure. A guy'll be here in a couple of minutes, but he didn't say what was going on."

Her arms went around her middle in what I recognized as a defensive thing. She was worried. "Do you think it could have something to do with Royse, or my mom?"

I considered my answer carefully before I spoke. "It could, or might be something completely different." As much as I hoped it would be the news she wanted, I couldn't give her false hope.

Her shoulders slumped a little. "Oh. Okay." Tears shimmered in her eyes before she looked away. "Um, I guess I should wait in there?" She gestured toward the bedroom.

"Not unless you'd rather not meet a guy called Stella." I laughed a little to try and ease her discomfort. "If it's something private, he'll let me know."

She nodded, still looking out of sorts. "Okay."

The buzzer for the security door sounded louder than usual. I hit the Open button without checking. If someone other than Stella showed up at my door in a minute, I'd blow their ass away. On that note, I grabbed my old .38 and thumbed the hammer back. The revolver had been with me through thick and thin, and was always my go-to.

A sharp knock came at the door, and I checked before opening it. As Stella came inside, I checked the hallway behind him, and closed the door, sliding the deadbolt home. I waved him toward the living room as I gently lowered the hammer and returned the gun to its place.

"What's up, man? Need a beer?"

"Yeah, could use one." Stella dropped into the chair nearest the door and stretched his legs out. He cast a significant glance at Elena as she hurried toward the kitchen.

I turned to grab him a beer, only to meet Elena already coming back with it. At my nod, she passed him the bottle, staying as far away as possible, then crossing her arms over her middle again.

"Stella, this is Elena, the girl I told you about last night." I took my usual seat on the couch and motioned for her to sit beside me.

Stella narrowed his eyes a little, and twisted the cap off his beer. "Good to meet you." He drained half the bottle in one swallow, then shook his head. "You done it up right, this time, Ryker. Got yourself a bounty on your head."

"Do I, now? Who's payin'?" The news really came as no

surprise. After I spoke to Luke, I hadn't expected Royse to just let my little adventure last night go. He had to make an example to make sure no one else got any ideas about him being soft.

"Royse's men put the word out, but he's not footing the bill. That's coming from Nikolai Bessanov. Seems Royse has some friends in high, or rather, very low, places."

"Mob?"

He nodded and finished his beer. "Looks that way. And some of the names that are coming back to me are a little familiar. I think there's a tie-in to the ones Vicki brought down on us."

The air left my lungs in a rush. I'd speculated the same thing earlier, but to have someone else come to the same conclusion came as a shock. That meant the connections existed somewhere other than just in my head. "I wondered about that. Why would they be here?"

"I don't know yet, but I've got feelers out. I'll let you know when I come up with any info. In the meantime, keep your head down. And keep her hid good." He gestured toward Elena. "They put a kill-on-sight hit on her."

Fuck.

Chapter Ten

Elena:

Kill on sight. The words echoed through my head as the man called Stella got to his feet and headed for the door. Ryker followed, and I could hear them speaking softly, but whatever they said meant nothing to me.

What the hell did *kill on sight* mean? Was it really as bad as it sounded? I hoped not.

The door clicked shut behind Stella as he left, and Ryker spent a moment fiddling with locks and a security panel. He came toward me, a dark frown creasing his forehead.

"You okay?" He sat and pulled me close.

I shook my head. "What did that mean?"

He sighed and lowered his head a little. "It means Royse is pissed at us both."

"You don't have to sugar-coat it. He's going to have me killed, isn't he?" Saying the words out loud turned my stomach. After all this time, that meant he would rather have me dead than give up any of his control over me. And if Ryker happened to get killed in the meantime, he was cool with that, too.

Ryker nodded. "Yeah, that's what he wants. I won't let it happen, though. You're safe." He wrapped both arms around me and rested his chin on top of my head. "I got you."

Sitting there, with Ryker holding me, I felt completely safe, for probably the first time since I was a kid. But logically, I knew he was only one man. Royse had a whole crew just waiting to do whatever he wanted. Ryker would try, but he couldn't keep me from them forever.

"I can't ask you to do this." I pushed away a little, not

sure where I was going to go.

"You're not asking me to do anything." He cupped my jaw in one big hand and gently forced me to look at him. "I could have turned away last night, and I don't know why I didn't, but I was going to help you even before you asked. I was there looking for you, instead of in the locker room where I belonged."

Looking for me? "What do you mean?" How could he have known I was there?

"When I came out, waiting to be called for the fight, I spotted you in the crowd. I saw the way that man was treating you, and I didn't like it. I'd gone to ask Royse where you were." The rumble of his voice, the words he spoke, sent thoughts whirling through my head.

In that moment I knew what I had to do. It would take time, and care, because if I made him suspicious, he might stop me. So I leaned back in and let him cradle me to his chest. The stupid tears kept trying to come, but I forced them back. I could do this, and I could keep it from him.

When he tipped my head back to kiss me again, I gave myself over to it. My luck sure proved itself once more. The moment I had something good in my life, something came along to take it away. Ryker might not want more than a few nights with me, but even with that, he was still the best thing to ever happen to me. And now Royse was going to take him away.

Ryker's kisses made me ache, both with a kind of need that felt totally new to me, and with grief. I wanted to spend forever right there in his arms, safe and secure in the knowledge he would never hurt me.

Crazy thinking. Men like him did not tie themselves down forever to whores. They had hookups and flings until they found a nice girl to settle down and have kids with. Sadness for what I would never have brought more tears for me to force back.

He deepened his kiss, bringing all my attention to the way his tongue coaxed mine. His beard stubble prickled slightly against my skin, making me even more aware of him. What would my life have been like if my mother hadn't got sick? Would I have a man like him to call my own?

Ryker brought one hand under the edge of my shirt and skimmed it over my belly, taking my thoughts away from what might have been and putting them on nothing but him and what he was doing. Just as well. I needed to focus on the here and now, instead of whining about some hazy half-baked dreams. When he carried me to his bed again, I was more than ready.

***

When I woke, I stretched, every part of my body still aware of Ryker's touch. He'd left the bed already, but the sheets were still warm on his side, so probably not long ago. Reluctant to leave the safe little world he created around me, I climbed out of bed, and pulled on my discarded clothes. I'd have to see about getting something else to wear. I couldn't very well just keep wearing those forever.

The thought of a hot shower led me toward the bathroom, but a noise just beyond drew me further. A door that always stayed closed stood open, allowing me to see inside what I'd assumed was a closet.

A mostly empty room lay before me, nearly as large as the bedroom. Ryker lay on a mat torturing himself with a difficult looking version of ab crunches. Sweat glistened on his bare shoulders and he grunted with effort. I backed out, not wanting to interrupt, and headed for that shower.

The hot water loosened my muscles and soothed the minor aches from my active night. I washed, using Ryker's masculine smelling shower gel and shampoo. What I normally used was far from fancy, but it at least had a slightly flowery scent. Maybe I could get to a dollar store sometime before I put my plan into action, and get something a little feminine.

As soon as the thought came, I shoved it away. I would need money to get anything, and I wouldn't be around long enough to bother with it anyway. No sense wasting money on stuff that would just sit there in the bottle forever.

The steam insulated me from the rest of the world, and I wasted a few minutes just enjoying it. If only all my problems would fade away in the steam. No such luck, though. I needed to suck it up and get on with what I had to do.

I finally shut the water off and dried myself, and kept a towel around my hair. Another towel practically swallowed me as I wrapped it around my body and tucked an edge in to hold it in place.

I found Ryker in the kitchen. "Hi."

He looked around, a little startled. "Hey. Did I wake you?"

"No, I just woke up." Keeping my eyes off his bare chest became a real struggle. I could look at him for hours and never get tired of it. "I hate to ask, but do you happen to have another shirt and shorts I could borrow?"

"Oh, yeah, of course. Sorry, I should have realized... I'll have Stella pick up a few things for you, if you'll give me a list."

I shook my head. "I can't ask you to do that. If he could go by my place, he could just grab my stuff there."

"No, can't do that. Royse probably has someone keeping an eye on your place. We can't have anyone following Stella back here and finding you."

Well, that made sense, even if I hated to admit it. I shrugged a little. "Then I guess I'm wearing your shorts and T-shirts. I don't have money for clothes and stuff."

The look he gave me meant something, but I wasn't sure what. "Don't worry about it. I have it covered."

"No. I don't want you spending money on me. Staying

here, and putting you in danger, is bad enough." It took everything I had not to just walk out his door and let him get back to his life.

"You don't understand, Elena." He caught my arms and prevented me from pulling away. "I have friends who are willing to help. Stella isn't going to the mall and buy a whole wardrobe. He'll give your list to one of our friends' girlfriends, and have them go to a second-hand store for most of it."

Okay, that didn't sound so bad. "So you're not spending a fortune?"

He grinned. "I'd like to. Unfortunately, I'll have to make my fortune first." One hand left my arm to cup my jaw. "Don't worry, okay?"

"Okay. If you say so." Of course, I would keep right on worrying.

"I do. Now, let's get you something clean to put on, and then you can make your list." He led the way to his room, where he quickly found another T-shirt and more drawstring shorts.

Ryker left me to get dressed, returning to the kitchen. When I came out, he had a pad and pen waiting. I frowned and wrote down my sizes while he worked on something at the counter.

"Make sure to add what kind of shampoo and stuff you like, along with whatever other girly stuff you'll need in the next few weeks."

I stared at his with a raised brow. "Girly stuff?"

He shrugged. "I don't know. Tampons and stuff."

Heat flooded my face. I hadn't thought that far ahead. That part of the list was pretty easy. I wasn't picky about brands and all that. I had to just get the cheap kind. "Okay, all done."

"You put shoes and underwear?"

I added those things to the bottom of the page. "I did now."

A chuckle rumbled from him. "Good girl. Now,

something else." He turned and put his hands on his hips. "I've been thinking. If we have to leave here, we don't need you being recognized. I think maybe you should think about dying your hair."

"Will we have to go somewhere else?" Alarm quickened my pulse. As long as we remained in the city, I could put my plan into action. If he took me too far away, I might as well forget it.

"It's possible, depending on how Royse reacts to our disappearing, and on what my friends find out about him. And if it takes more than a few days to get things sorted out and find your mom, it'll be easier if we're somewhere else."

"Oh. Okay." I weighed the idea. Looking different might actually let me put my plan into effect sooner. "I always wanted to be a redhead."

His turn to raise a brow. "A redhead? Really?" He grinned. "Well, hopefully we can make that happen."

The rest of the day passed in eating, watching TV, having sex, and talking. Mostly talking, which surprised me more than a little. Most of my experience with men led me to believe they wanted sex from a woman, and not much else. Especially not conversation.

But it seemed Ryker was different. We talked about everything under the sun, including our childhoods, the foods we loved, and how we liked to spend time. For me, that last part was a small category. Okay, all of them were. I hadn't been able to try new foods in a long time, always forced to grab the cheapest things on the store shelves. And my time hadn't belonged to me since my mom got sick.

Late in the evening, his phone buzzed, and Stella arrived. He only came in for a moment, long enough to pass Ryker a canvas bag stuffed to the brim, and a handful of plastic shopping bags. They talked quietly, then Stella offered a half-wave in my direction, and left.

Ryker brought the canvas bag, and some of the shopping bags over to me. "Here's the clothes and stuff the girls picked up for you. Stella said these two bags are for you, too. I had him pick up some groceries, too, so I'll be in the kitchen while you check out what they sent you."

As much as I hadn't wanted Ryker to spend money on me, I couldn't contain the excitement at getting new things. My hands shook like crazy when I took the bags from him. I didn't wait, just dumped the canvas bag on the couch.

Disbelief made my eyes water. Jeans, cute tops, a hoodie, two pairs of shoes, and even a dress spread before me. I didn't know what to think, or say. I sat touching the clothes, enjoying the fabrics, for a long time. They might have come from secondhand shops, but they were far nicer than anything I'd ever owned.

I finally managed to fold everything into a neat stack, and turned for the other bags. One had a store logo on the side, but I didn't recognize it. Inside, three pretty, lacy bras with matching panties, several pairs of socks, tank tops and shorts, along with a pair of silky pajama pants, waited. Tears rolled down my cheeks. Never, not in my wildest dreams, had I ever imagined having things like these.

The thought of opening the third bag terrified me. It came from a different store, the logo on the bag also unfamiliar. Unable to resist, I carefully opened the top and looked inside. Shampoo, conditioner and shower gel in bright bottles certainly looked nothing like the dollar store brands I asked for on the list. Beyond those, I found lotion, razors, a hairbrush and blow dryer, and even a pack of bands to put my hair up with.

Still, the bag held more. They'd thought of everything, including makeup that suited my coloring, and the hair dye kit. By the time I finished taking all the stuff out, I had more feminine products than I even knew real women actually used.

I sat there on the floor, with all the treasures spread

around me. When the sobs came, I didn't even try to hold them back. Gratitude flooded through me. How could these women who didn't even know me take the time and care to pick out such nice things for me? Not to mention the money they must have spent. The whole thing boggled my mind.

Chapter Eleven

Ryker:

I stood there in helpless silence as Elena cried. I'd come in to tell her Stella had included ice cream with the groceries, if she wanted some. Instead, I found her bawling, and had no clue what might be wrong. Unless I missed my guess, Stella probably asked Vicki to pick up the things Elena needed. A few of the Hell Raiders had girlfriends or ol' ladies, but Kellen's wife tended to be the one who took care of anything that needed a woman's touch.

Finally, Elena seemed to quiet a little. "What's wrong?" Once more, surprise hit. I actually wanted to know, and to fix, the problem. For a woman as strong as Elena to break down like that, it must be something serious.

She looked up, startled, and hurried to wipe her tears away. "Nothing. I'm sorry, I didn't mean to disturb you."

I went to her and dropped to my knees at her side. Her hair had fallen forward, hiding her face from me, and I pushed it back. "Elena, come on. I can help."

She smiled through the tears. "Really, nothing is wrong." She gestured at the things sitting around her. "I've never had anything this nice before."

Nothing as nice as some thrift store clothes and normal female stuff? Suddenly, I felt incredibly sad for her. Life had been far from easy for her. I barely stopped myself from telling her I would get her beautiful clothes, shoes, and whatever else she wanted.

Instead, I found a way to get her mind off her tears. An emerald green bra and panty set caught my attention and I lifted it out of the pile. "Try it on for me?"

The shy expression she wore when she looked up at me made my stomach flip. "Why?"

Had no man ever asked to see her in something sexy? "Because I want to see that beautiful body in something hot, and then take it off and kiss every inch." Maybe that answer was a little blunt, but at least I didn't lie.

Her cheeks went a shade of pink that had nothing to do with crying. "Really?"

"Really." I took her hand and brought it to the front of my pants as proof. "See? I can't wait."

She gave my half-hard dick a little squeeze. "Okay, then." Blushing furiously, she rose and left the room.

This woman had me all tied in knots. What was it about her? Even as I asked myself, I knew. Circumstances forced her into turning tricks, but for all that, she seemed as innocent as a virgin in some ways. She hadn't had a chance to learn to be around a man beyond sex. That made me wonder if she'd ever enjoyed it with her johns. Not like I could ask, though.

All I could do was make damn sure she liked every single time with me. I'd never gone too far out of my way to make sure a chick I fucked got off. Sure, I liked it when they did, and I took the time to make sure they were ready or whatever, but it never seemed all that important. Suddenly, I wanted to use everything I knew about sex to make Elena come repeatedly every single time I touched her.

A small sound drew my attention to the door. Elena stood there in her new bra and panties, halfway trying to cover herself, and blushing like crazy.

The sight hit me like a solid punch to the solar plexus. *Fuck!*

I caught my breath and managed to climb to my feet. "Fucking beautiful." For a minute, my legs refused to obey and kept me rooted to the spot.

She started to turn away, and I finally managed to move.

"Wait!" I grabbed her arm and turned her back. "Let me see you." Fuck, all that smooth golden skin and the luscious curves made my mouth go dry. Hell, I would beg if I had to, just to get a look at her.

Wide, dark eyes stared up at me with questions in them I didn't want to think about. So I lowered my head to taste those soft lips. Fuck, her mouth was incredible. A soft little moan came from her when I left her lips to taste the tender skin of her neck.

She moved in closer, arching her body to fit her curves to me while her hands clutched at my shoulders. I slid my hands down over her perfect hips and around to cup her ass, then a little lower to lift her. The wall seemed like a perfect place to take her, but I'd decided to make this about her, not me. The couch offered the closest surface to lay her on besides the floor, so I headed that way.

I took my time kissing her delicious mouth and exploring every dip and curve of her neck and shoulders. The new bra held her tits in a way that made me want nothing more than to stare and touch, and I drew it away almost reluctantly. Her nipples waited, flushed and pointed, for my attention as she made impatient sounds and thrust them at me. I finally gave her what she wanted and drew one into my mouth while I rolled the other between my thumb and finger. The moan she gave nearly undid my determination.

This time was all hers, I reminded myself, even if my dick wanted to dive right in. Continuing to lick and suck at her beautiful tits, I let one hand sweep down over her ribs, along the curve of her hip, until I found the lace of her panties. The fabric led my fingers to her mound and her breath hitched when I cupped her. Damp heat made my cock throb as I lightly brushed the tender flesh shielded by the little scrap of lace.

Elena moaned and wriggled, lifting her hips. A tiny bit

more pressure from my hand made her cry out and buck against me. Her responses to my touch and kisses were so incredible my chest tightened with pride. I was pretty sure no man had ever felt her heat this way before. Surprise at the realization I wanted to experience her this way for a very long time brought on a small hesitation.

The possibility of wanting her beyond the few days spent in her company as I helped her totally floored me. Already, I had fucked her more than any woman I could recall. I was normally a one and done kind of guy. Occasionally, a chick held my attention more than one night, but she had to be absolutely outstanding. Yet here I was, thinking in terms of a future with Elena; a future where I gave her everything she wanted and spent hours without end pleasing her body.

Her small cries as I kissed my way down her belly made me smile against her skin. I eased her knees further apart and settled my mouth over the silky lace that still covered her. The heady scent of her arousal caused my cock to jerk and want to be buried inside her. Once more, I reminded myself of the goal for this time. To show her as much pleasure as any one girl could experience.

I worked my mouth against her, pleased at the strangled cries she uttered. Abruptly, her hands found my head and her fingers raked through my hair. Impatient to taste all of her, I slid the panties off her, trailing my fingertips down the sensitive skin of her legs as I did.

Suddenly, she lay there before me, damp and ready, begging for my touch. My heart thudded hard against my chest as I leaned in for the first taste. A long, slow lick ended with circling her clit and a sharp cry from Elena. Her thighs tightened reflexively around my head and I looked up the length of her body to meet those dark eyes, heavy with desire. Her expression squeezed my hard-on like a physical touch.

I devoured her, licking, sucking, probing, and exploring

every secret, until she whimpered and bucked helpless under me. She hovered at the edge of orgasm, her body vibrating with need. If I could keep her right there in that moment for the rest of my life, I would die a happy man. She probably wouldn't be all that happy with me, though, if the frustrated noises she kept making were anything to judge by.

I smiled against her and slipped one finger into her slick heat. Her muscles clutched hard and her back arched to pull me deeper. I drew my hand back a little, teasing, then thrust deep to stroke her inner walls. At the same time, I sucked her clit into my mouth and hummed.

Elena's body locked tight and a shrill cry tore from her throat. Tight inner muscles contracted hard, even as I continued to stroke and flick my tongue. I kept going until she shifted and half-heartedly pushed me away.

The sight of her laid out for me, body lax and sated, with a light sheen of sweat over that smooth golden skin, seared itself into my mind. After this, I realized how Kellen, Trip, and some of the other Hell Raiders were so pussy-whipped. At that moment, I would do anything and everything to bring that glow to Elena's body again.

How the hell did a man get into so much trouble? There was absolutely no question I would never be the same again.

And then she reached for me. "Please, Ryker, I need you."

Alarm pounded through my veins. "Are you okay?" Had I hurt her?

She wound her legs around my waist and tugged, pulling me close. "I need you inside me."

My dick throbbed as I eagerly filled her request and sank into her sweet body. She writhed under me, pulling me deeper while her nails raked over my shoulders. An unreasonable need to take my time, make it last, and make her come again hit, and I held still, trying to stave off my own orgasm.

Elena had other ideas, though. She arched, rippling around me. "Please, Ryker."

The breathless words sent sparks of need racing along my skin, and left me helpless to resist. I thrust, hard and deep. Within seconds, I pounded into Elena, and she gave a sharp cry every time I slammed into her.

A massive explosion gathered at the base of my spine, ready to tear me to bits. Elena's body wrapped around me in a spasm of pleasure as she tumbled over the edge into another orgasm, and took me with her.

Somehow, I managed to find Earth again as I came back down. My lungs struggled to pull in enough air while my muscles trembled with the strain of keeping my weight off Elena.

She smiled up at me with something like wonder in her eyes. "What did you do to me?"

I chuckled and allowed myself to collapse to her side, so we ended up sprawled side-by-side on the couch. "I don't know, but whatever it was, you did it to me, too." Who knew some thrift shop clothes and normal female things would get me the best sex of my life?

I sobered as my breathing returned to something like normal. What the hell was I going to do when we found her mom and got Royse off her back?

Chapter Twelve

Elena:

I had the feeling my life was about to get even more complicated. Ryker carried me to the shower and washed me with my new stuff. I never dreamed a man could be that gentle or sweet. Especially not a man like Ryker, a fighter with the bruises and scrapes of his last match still marking his perfect body. When he finished, he brought one of my new tank tops and a pair of shorts for me to put on.

When I came out of the bathroom, I felt more feminine, more cherished, than I ever dreamed possible. Women like me didn't get to live that life, and I dreaded returning to my real one. Part of me wanted to stay right there with Ryker, waiting, forever. Then the guilt set in. If time stood still and let me stay there with him, my mom would never have a chance of getting away from Royse.

No matter how much I wanted to forget everything that existed outside his apartment, I couldn't. My mom deserved better than that. I had to do whatever it took to get her back. At least now that I had clothes and a way to disguise myself, I stood a chance of carrying out my plan to save both her and Ryker.

After his own shower, Ryker held me on the couch and we watched a movie. Absorbed with plotting my getaway, I couldn't follow the story. When the movie ended, Ryker excused himself to cook.

"While you do that, if it's okay, I'll dye my hair. Do you have some scissors and maybe a couple of old towels?"

"That sounds like a plan." He brought me his T-shirt and

shorts. "Might want to put these on so you don't get it on your stuff." While I changed, he brought scissors and two faded towels with the emblem of a gym printed at the edge.

I learned to cut my own hair long ago, since even a cheap cut cost more than I could afford. Luckily, I always kept my hair in long layers, so I had something to work with. The dye intimidated the hell out of me, but I went over the directions carefully and followed them exactly.

After all the timing, rinsing, conditioning, and drying, I studied my reflection critically. My hair fell in deep auburn waves over my shoulders, a couple of shades darker than I expected. I was tempted to leave it the same length, but in the end, decided not to take the chance. By the time I finished, my hair was far shorter than I'd ever worn it, but I thought it looked okay. I cleaned up the mess, then fussed with my hair a few more minutes before putting my tank top and shorts back on.

Several times during my makeover, Ryker tapped at the closed bathroom door and asked if I needed help. I refused, determined to keep what distance I could from him. Already, I was way too close, and wanted so much more. If I had any hope of getting out of this, I needed to keep my heart separate from him.

Finished and unable to put off going out any longer, I opened the bathroom door and took a deep breath. Rich, tantalizing smells led me the kitchen, where I found Ryker slicing vegetables, maybe for a salad, and stood watching him for a minute. He'd dressed in a pair of soft-looking cotton pajama pants that hung low on his hips, and a thread-bare gray wife-beater that emphasized the breadth of his shoulders.

Seeing him like that made my mouth go dry with want.

He heard me and turned. I stood, uncomfortable and nervous, as he took in the changes. That gaze swept over me and left me feeling bare as his eyes darkened with desire. "Still beautiful, baby girl." He smiled a little. "I don't think anybody would recognize you now, at least not without a close look. When we have to go out, you should be safe." His words filled me with relief.

"I'm glad. I hoped it would be enough." One step closer to carrying out my plan. Maybe I could even get close before Royse discovered what I was doing.

"Dinner will be ready in a couple of minutes, if you want to grab plates. Okay with you if we eat in front of the TV? I noticed the movie earlier didn't keep your attention, so this time it's your choice." He grinned, once more showing the sweet considerate side that seemed so out of place.

I laughed a little. "Works for me. You ready for a chick-flick?"

He clutched at his chest and made a funny face. "Oh, my God, anything but that!" He pretended to stumble. Grabbing my hand, he pulled me into his arms and brushed my hair back. "Whatever you want, baby girl." Suddenly serious, he lowered his head to claim my mouth.

Distance. I needed to keep my distance. Otherwise, I wouldn't have the strength to carry out my plan. Falling in love with him didn't work. In self-defense, I ducked away with a laugh. "Oh, no, you don't. I'm starved, and I'm so holding you to the movie."

Ryker's laughter followed me to the cabinet where I took out the plates. "I hope you like Chinese." He tossed the sliced vegetables into a hot pan, where they sizzled while he moved them around. "I don't normally eat it, but I figure I've shot my nutrition plan all to hell already this week, one more meal won't hurt."

He heaped white rice on both plates, added the vegetables, and topped it with chunks of meat in a thick sauce, then added noodles to one side. The oven timer dinged and he hurried to take a pan out.

"I cheated with frozen egg rolls, but hopefully they'll be

good." He added two of the crispy golden rolls to each plate.

My stomach growled loudly in appreciation. I had no idea whether I liked Chinese food. "I'm sure I'll love it."

He glanced up at me in surprise and waited for an explanation.

I gave a little shrug. "I've never really had Chinese before, unless you count Ramen noodles."

He nodded. "Well, hopefully you'll like it. And after we eat, maybe you'll tell me what kinds of food you like so we can have those, too. I'm not used to taking anybody else's likes and dislikes into consideration." He passed me one of the plates. "I'll grab drinks if you'll get forks and napkins."

I nodded and reached for the drawer. "I doubt you'd like the kinds of things I usually have." Since I'd known him, Ryker always ate real food. "Canned soups, frozen pizza, Ramen noodles. Whatever's cheap and easy. I don't have much of a way to actually cook at my place, or money for food. Mostly I just grab a couple of things from the dollar store."

Ryker stayed silent, pouring something from a pitcher into glasses of ice. When he looked up, he nodded. "I remember times like that when I was a kid. My grandparents helped us, but there was never enough money to go around, so we skimped where we could. I'm sorry you had to go through that." His quiet voice wrapped around me in a comforting blanket.

God, I had to be careful. He was too good. I reminded myself again to keep him at a distance. "It's no big deal. I'm used to it." Going back to my old life would not be easy after the way he spoiled me. I needed to keep that fact front and center in my mind. He was not mine, and when this was over, I had to go back. If I survived.

He handed me a glass of amber liquid and took his fork and napkin, then picked up his plate and led the way to the couch. He sat and dragged the coffee table closer with his foot hooked under the edge. Drink and plate on the table, he sat up to take mine and put them beside his. The expression he wore was more serious than I'd seen him lately.

"Elena, there's a lot about your life I wish had been different. But then I think, if you hadn't gone through what you did, I might not have met you." He raised one hand to tuck a few strands of hair behind my ear. "And I'm really glad we met." He looked at me for a minute, staring into my eyes. "Okay, let's eat before it gets cold."

He didn't give me time to consider his words, passing me the remote and ordering me to choose something for us to watch. I finally settled on a movie about a woman who moved to a new town after her husband left her, and fell in love with her new neighbor.

I rarely had the chance to really watch TV, but when I did, I always wished I could have the life of one of the characters. And suddenly, I did. At least for a short time.

The food turned out to be delicious. The tender bits of chicken were breaded and soaked in a rich, sweet sauce. The eggrolls were totally unexpected, with bits of meat and other things mixed with chopped cabbage inside the crispy shells. I didn't even question where the eggs were. The sweet tea went with it all perfectly. By the time my plate was empty, the movie had reached the halfway point.

I sat back, amazed that I'd eaten so much. The food on my plate for that one meal probably amounted to more than I ate in an average week. "If you keep feeding me like this, I'm going to be big as a whale."

Ryker laughed at my fake complaint. "I guess you better start working out, then, because I intend to keep feeding you."

My heart thumped as I forced my attention back to the movie, refusing to say anything more. We sat there, side by side, and watched the movie in silence, though I noticed Ryker watched me more than the TV.

His phone rang as the movie ended, and I turned the TV

off and took the dishes to the kitchen while he spoke quietly to whoever was on the other end of the call. I carefully avoided listening in, and cleaned up from the meal.

As I finished up, he came into the kitchen and leaned one hip against the counter. "That was Stella. We need to move tonight."

Shock left me speechless. "Why?"

"We have information that Royse is planning to send his men here, with orders to bring you back. So as soon as it gets dark, we'll be out of here. If they manage to get in, they'll find us long gone."

Panic surged. If we left, I couldn't do what I'd planned. At least, not easily. "Where will we go?" The answer to that question would determine how hard I would have to work.

He hesitated for a second, making me wonder if he even knew. "We're going over the river to a little town in Kentucky. Stags Leap. I have connections there. We'll be safe."

"Connections?" That word reminded me of drug dealers.

He sighed. "I'm a full member of the Hell Raiders MC. We're based in Stags Leap. That's where you and I are going."

Oh, shit. I didn't know what to say. I should have known, considering the motorcycle and the leather vest he wore. But I hadn't gotten a look at it before, and the idea of anyone I knew, even slightly, being part of the Hell Raiders seemed far-fetched.

They were well-known throughout the area for being dangerous to cross. No one really knew what kind of illegal things they were involved in, and I didn't want to know. Fear raised goose bumps on my arms. I'd gone from the frying pan right into the fire.

Chapter Thirteen

Ryker:

She was hiding something. She kept a distance between us and guarded her words. If I had to guess, I'd say she planned to go off the rez and do something rash about Royse on her own. I couldn't let her do that. Royse and his men would eat her alive.

When I had a chance to talk to Stella and Kellen about it, they suggested moving her to the clubhouse. It only made sense, with Royse's men hitting all the gyms hard looking for me. They knew I could only go so long before getting back into training, or I would have to kiss my career goodbye. The limited workouts I could do at home weren't going to keep me in fighting form. So I agreed to the move.

The fear in Elena's eyes when I told her about the Hell Raiders bothered me. I knew we had a less than wonderful rep among most people in the area, but for someone to actually fear us seemed extreme. But then I thought about it. The Hell Raiders ran Stags Leap and the surrounding area, and guarded it fiercely. We played hard in the nearby towns, and let some of our business spill over into them. Yeah, fear probably fit the bill.

Either way, I had to get Elena to a safer place and where she couldn't go after Royse on her own. I helped her get all her new stuff packed, and threw a few things of my own into a bag. I already had stuff at the clubhouse, but with no idea how long we'd have to stay, I'd rather not leave things to chance.

We cleaned everything up, since I'd rather not come home to dirty laundry and spoiled stuff in the fridge. By the time we finished all that, Elena got dressed. The jeans fit her like a glove and the top she picked hugged her tits and made my hands ache to touch.

"We'd better hit the road, before I peel those clothes off you and remind myself how that body feels wrapped around me." I meant every word.

Her eyes widened with surprise, then she gave a little laugh. "I guess we should go then." She grabbed the bag with her stuff before I had a chance to, and headed for the door.

I led her down to the garage and put our stuff in the Chevelle. Leaving my bike behind made my chest tight, but there really wasn't a choice. Besides, I'd already arranged for Dix and a prospect to pick it up later in the night.

The stunned look on Elena's face as she took in the car made up for the tight chest. "This is yours?"

I grinned. "Yeah. Took forever to restore her."

"It's amazing." She ran a fingertip along the fender.

"Thanks." I opened the passenger door for her and waited for her to get in, then closed it. As I rounded the hood, I caught a glimpse of her face as she took in the interior. I'd kept the exterior original, but had to make a few modifications inside. Still, climbing into that car was like stepping back through time, and Elena looked like she'd just woke up in 1970.

I started her up and let the engine growl, pleased with Elena's gasp. The armrest and dashboard would probably have permanent imprints from her fingernails, with the way she hung on when I put the car in gear and pulled out of the parking garage. That made me wonder what she'd do when I blew past one-twenty on the river bottom straight stretches. I smiled at the thought.

We made it out of town without trouble, but as soon as we crossed the bridge, I noticed a big jacked up pickup following too close. The only outlet for the damn bridge consisted of a rural two-lane, so when I turned right and the truck followed, I had no options for several miles but to stay ahead of him. The first left after the bridge led into a narrow hollow between the mountains, and I took it.

The truck stayed right on my bumper, but with a couple dozen houses along the hollow, I still had no way of knowing for sure whether he followed me. Halfway through, I pulled into the lot of a rural church, whipped the car around, and headed back down toward the main road. My suspicions proved out when the truck copied my move and accelerated to catch up again.

"Elena, I need you to stay down and stay calm. We're being followed." Sure, it might have been easier to not say anything, but I needed her to be ready in case of trouble.

"Oh, God. I should have just gone to Royse and gave in to whatever he wanted."

Her words chilled me to the bone. "What do you mean?" Even with just the dim glow from the dash, I could see the tears rolling down her cheeks.

She wiped them away and took a deep breath. "When he had my mom taken, I should have gone to him right away. If I'd just done what he wanted, none of this would have happened."

I stayed quiet, totally floored by her way of thinking. Instead, I concentrated on driving and keeping that bastard in the pickup off my bumper. With a lower center of gravity, and probably more horsepower, my car could leave him in the dust on the crooked road. I took it easy, though, well aware what could happen if I took a curve just a hair too tight or too loose.

When I made the turn back out on the main road, though, it was a different story. I'd driven that stretch thousands of times, in all sorts of conditions. Every dip and sway stayed fixed in my mind, and I knew all the sweet spots that would allow me to take the curves at full speed. I gambled on the truck driver not knowing it.

The big 454 roared as I gave it more gas, and the car

shot ahead. The truck's headlights grew smaller in the rearview until I rounded a curve, then disappeared altogether. I kept the hammer down and gained as much ground as I could while they were out of sight.

Beside me, Elena clutched at the seat. "Ryker, really, just turn around and take me home. I'll go to Royse and fix all this."

I bit back a curse. Scaring her would only create more problems. "Look, Elena, he was going to have you killed. When the sick fucks he sent you to couldn't do it, he gave you to a bastard that never returns the girls he gets. Why do you think going to him now would fix anything?" My fingers tightened on the steering wheel so hard I had to remind myself to be careful and not crack it. I took another curve, almost impossibly tight, and she gave a little squeal.

When she could breathe again, she replied. "The whole thing was my fault. I shouldn't have found a job or tried to leave. If I go back and do as he wants, he'll get his way. That's all he wants."

Frustration tightened my hands again. "No, Elena, that is not all he wants. He wants us both dead now. We dared to go against him. No amount of apologizing or doing what he wants is going to fix that."

She made an angry sound. "I have to try, Ryker. We can't hide or run forever, and he still has my mom if he hasn't killed her yet. There's no other way." Her small fist pounded at her thigh. "You have to let me do this."

I hit the gas harder and took the next curve with screaming tires. "No! Even if you went back, he would just kill you, kill your mom, and keep coming after me. It's too late. You have to believe me."

She laughed, a bitter sound. "He's going to kill me anyway. It's easier just to get it over with."

"Damn it, Elena. Listen to me. I can keep you safe. The

Hell Raiders—"

"Are more blood-thirsty criminals, probably worse than Royse. How is that going to be any better?" The interruption left me stunned.

I kept my eyes on the road, trying to let it sink in. How could she think the Raiders were worse than Royse? It made no sense. Down a long straight stretch, I floored it and let the car surge ahead. Just as I started around the next curve, headlights appeared in my rearview. The truck was hanging in there.

"I don't know what you've heard about the Raiders, but we're nothing like Royse. For one thing, we don't make money by selling women who don't want to be sold. And we don't hurt women."

She stayed quiet and I didn't say anything else. Best to keep my attention on driving. The worst part of the road was coming right at us, and I had to stay focused to take it at this speed. The slightest mistake would save Royse the trouble of killing us.

We reached the town before Stags Leap well ahead of the pickup. Well, at least the headlights were nowhere to be seen. I took a deep breath of relief. From here, I had a choice of over a dozen ways out of town, all leading to different places. The bastards following us would have no clue which way we took. I felt a little better about our chances of getting out alive.

"Ryker?" Elena's voice sounded small and scared.

"Yeah?"

"Could we maybe stop for a minute? I really need the bathroom."

I took a quick look in my rearview. No sign of that truck. Shit, I hated to give up our lead on them, but it couldn't really be helped. We had over an hour left on the road, and I couldn't ask her to hold it that long. "Okay, I'll find a place to stop."

The next cross street led to a less visible part of town,

down next to the River, so I hung a right and headed that way. Three streets later, next to the ancient abandoned ferry landing, a little mom and pop convenience store/gas station/diner looked like the perfect solution. I parked in the shadows near the dumpster and led Elena inside.

While she headed for the restroom, I grabbed some drinks and snacks, knowing we would need it when we reached the clubhouse. I paid and waited, wondering how long a woman usually took in the restroom.

Five minutes passed, and my nerves got the better of me. "Hey, does the ladies room have another exit?" Surely she wouldn't ditch me and try to get back to Royse after our talk?

"Nah, man, just a window for ventilation." The clerk gave me a weird look, but then turned back to his cellphone and continued his mindless game.

A sick feeling hit my gut. Shit. She wouldn't, would she?

I ran to the ladies room and forced the door without knocking. A cool breeze came in through the open window, and Elena was nowhere to be seen.

Fuck!

I ran through the store and straight-armed the door open, then jogged to the left, out of the lights. There I paused for a look around, hoping to catch a glimpse of Elena. No such luck. Damn, she couldn't just make it easy on me and listen to reason, could she? No, that would make too much fucking sense.

Chapter Fourteen

Elena:

This might be the stupidest thing I've ever done. I bent down beside the gas station to get my bearings. Royse's men were probably long gone, so I needed to make my way back across the River by myself. But first, I had to make sure Ryker didn't find me.

A little shiver of fear ran through me. Pissing off a man like him couldn't be a good thing. I ignored the little voice in the back of my mind that kept saying Ryker would never hurt me, even pissed. Regret filled me, for leaving all my new things behind. I would miss them, even if I hadn't had time to get used to having them.

Thick shadows at the edge of the parking lot seemed like the way to go, so I headed in that direction, trying to hurry. At the curb, moonlight glinted off water just in time to keep me from stepping right in it. I paused to take a better look at where I was going, and it was a good thing. The water I'd glimpsed stretched before me in a broad sort of channel between two concrete walls, like a boat ramp or something. Huge iron rings protruded from the walls; maybe a place to tie boats?

Either way, it was a damn good thing I'd seen that little sparkle of water. Who knew how deep it was right there. I could have drowned. Panic hit for a minute, but I took a deep breath to calm down. Every second it took me to get back to Royse was another second Ryker could get killed. I might be nothing but a nasty whore, but I couldn't stand the thought of his death, especially not because of me.

Another deep breath to get me on my way, and I skirted

around the curb, and made my way to the street. The need to
stay out of Ryker's sight warred with wanting to find the men in
the truck and an easy way back to Royse. I decided out of sight
was better. I could find my way back to Royse, as long as Ryker
didn't find me first.

The first alley I found seemed like it might offer what I
needed, so I headed down it carefully. I already knew way too
much about the kinds of monsters that lurked in alleys, even in
little Mayberry-looking towns like this one. Luckily, though,
this one seemed like just rear entrance access for the houses to
both sides. A dog barked, and another answered, but both went
quiet soon, probably bored with me.

The problem came when I made it to the end of the
alley. It fucking dead-ended, and not just any dead-end with a
fence or building, or whatever. No, this one had some big-ass
forest cutting it off. To my left, moonlight sparkled off a big
body of water, probably the River. Double railroad tracks sat off
to my right, with more gigantic trees on the other side.

That forest would swallow me alive, and the choices in
front of me turned my stomach. Risk walking along the River at
night, with no way of seeing snakes, or dead bodies, or
whatever else I might stumble into; or take my chances with the
railroad and get mowed down by a freight train in the night. The
other option held even less appeal. I *could* retrace my steps and
find another way out of town, but that meant more chances of
Ryker finding me.

All three choices sucked, but in the end, Ryker scared
me far less than dead bodies and snakes, or silent trains that
killed. I headed back the way I came, watching between the
houses for another street or alley I could try. Something scurried
around a trash can, and scared me half to death. My little half-
scream might have started the dog barking again, or maybe it
was more interested in whatever ran from the garbage.
Whichever, this time, it had a fit, and someone turned on a back

porch light and yelled for the dog to shut the fuck up. The dog whimpered and I got the hell out of there, as quietly as I could manage.

At the end of the alley, Ryker's car stood out clearly in the gas station lot, even if he had parked away from the lights. I could just walk over there and wait for him, let him go ahead and take the risk for me. It would be easier than what I'd decided on. He and his buddies could take the heat from Royse while I found myself somewhere to make a fresh start.

And what about mom? I froze, thinking. It wasn't the first time the idea had crossed my mind. Hell, I'd thought of ditching the old lady since the first time I had to beg for something to eat, and about a billion times since then. A few times, I'd even gone so far as to start to leave, but I always went back. No, I still couldn't leave her behind.

Decision made, I hurried and cut through a little park and found the street Ryker drove us down. It only took a few minutes from there to reach the edge of the little town, but was it the right edge? Not like I could stop and ask directions. Finally, I spotted a green road sign with the directions and distances to various other places. According to that, I had just over thirty miles to walk.

My heart sank at the thought, but then a car blasted by me, headed exactly where I needed to go. I spun to look behind me, and see if there might be more coming. Sure enough, headlights made me squint and throw one hand up to guard my eyes. Even so, I hurried and stuck my thumb out, willing the car to stop for me.

It did. The driver's window came down to show a young-looking guy. "Hey, doll, where ya headed?"

I told him, reminding myself of all the horrible things that happened to hitchhikers in the movies.

"Cool, I'm headed there to pick my wife up from work at the hospital. Climb in if you want a ride."

I weighed the risks for another full second and jogged across to the passenger side and climbed in. Before I could change my mind, I settled in and fastened my seat belt. After all, he was going to get his wife. She worked at the hospital.

He started driving. "I'm Brad, by the way." The glow from the dashboard made his smile look really nice.

"Elena." Shit, I realized too late I should have given him a fake name.

He nodded. "Elena. Cool name. You got friends in P-Town, or family?"

Uh oh. "Yeah, my mom and three brothers are there, and my boyfriend. I just came down here for the day with my friend, Beth, but she decided to stay the night, and I wanted to get home." Fuck, I hoped he didn't ask any more questions.

"Well, that sucks. Glad I stopped then." He seemed content with that, and turned his radio back up a little.

The dark scenery passed quickly, with blurs of light from the houses scattered along the way, and pretty soon, Brad turned onto the bridge across the River. From there, I asked him to drop me at the first cross street, since he had to go a different direction for the hospital.

The streets were quiet here in the business area, but I knew just a few blocks away, things were still jumping. The dealers and street whores would be out in force in the poorer neighborhoods, along with plenty of thugs. Maybe I would be lucky enough to get where I needed to go without trouble. A few blocks down, I saw that wasn't going to happen.

A thug pimp swaggered in my direction with two whores following after, probably searching for new territory. "Yo, bitch! Who your daddy?"

My breath froze in my chest, but I forced the words out anyway. "I'm with Royse, you dumb fuck. Now get the hell outta my way before one o' his boys moves you." Any woman walking alone in this area could count on getting asked that question at least once per block. The pimps were always on the lookout for fresh pussy.

A sly look passed between the whores, who hurried to catch up. "You ain't gon' let her talk to you like that, right El Chapo?" The peroxide blonde shoved her fake tits up against his arm

"Course I ain't." The so-called El Chapo glared at me. "I call bullshit, bitch. Royse don't run no street pussy."

I laughed. "El Chapo, is it? You're right, he don't. It's all private arrangement. You wanna call him and check?"

The punk held up both hands. "Nah, no need. I take your word."

"You sure? I can call him for you. Though he usually doesn't like his girls being questioned by two-bit hood rats." I reached for my pocket, like I had a phone there.

"No, seriously. We good, you know what I mean?" He backed away.

"Yeah, I know exactly what you mean." I walked on. The after-effects of fear made my palms itch. Stupid, but it never failed, the very center of my palms itched whenever I got upset or scared, but this was the first time lately I'd had a chance to even notice it. Being scared had been a long-term condition for me the last couple of weeks. This little confrontation had come off in my favor. Too bad the one with Royse wouldn't.

I kept moving, knowing without a doubt that to stand still was to become a victim in this neighborhood. My surroundings went from bad to worse, until gang graffiti tagged nearly every surface, and bits of trash blew along the sidewalk. Several panhandlers called out to me, asking for money I didn't have, so I ignored them. Only a single heartbeat kept me out of their shoes. A streetwalker wearing a shredded tank top that barely covered her nipples and shorts so short her ass cheeks hung out asked if I wanted a date. Nothing but Royse's protection separated me from her, and now I no longer had it. I figured I was lucky he would kill me.

It seemed like I walked forever before I reached Royse's building, but finally, I got there. Outside, it looked like an old fancy hotel or something, with all sorts of carvings and ornaments along the front. They'd even used two colors of stone when they built it, making a pretty pattern on the walls. A bronze plaque was fastened to one of the stones at the corner of the building, probably saying it was some kind of historic site or something. I'd never bothered to look that closely. No graffiti marked Royse's walls. The gangs knew better.

More nervous than I'd been the first time I saw that place, I made my way up the broad stone steps to the fancy double doors with their polished wood frames and brass handles. The full length glass was frosted in a pattern that imitated the ones the bricks made on the outside walls.

The itch in my palms became a full-on burning as I lifted a shaking hand to press the button by the doors. It wouldn't be long before I forgot to notice it again, because I would be too busy either fighting for my life, or being terrified. The old-fashioned bell rang inside, and I heard it clearly where I stood.

After a couple of minutes, a frowning man in a suit opened the right-hand door. "Yeah?"

I took a deep breath. "Elena, here to see Royse, please."

The man grinned and his gaze swept over me, missing nothing. "You're the split that caused so much bullshit? Well, come on in, darlin'. I'm sure Royse will be very pleased to see you."

My hands threatened to catch fire, and my heart seemed determined to leave my chest, but I stepped through the door. Ryker. I had to keep him safe. This was the only way. What happened to me didn't matter. I was only a whore anyway. I had to keep telling myself that or chicken out, and if I failed, Ryker would die. I couldn't face a world without him in it, so whatever happened to me here meant nothing, as long as he stayed okay.

Putting someone other than my mom before my own well-being felt entirely strange. I never went out of my way to hurt anyone, of course, but I didn't go out of my way to help anyone, either. But for Ryker, I would do anything possible to keep him safe, even if it meant my own death, or worse. I'd realized it earlier, of course, and set myself to do it, but having my feelings put into actual words did something to my insides.

I stepped through those fancy doors and waited for my fate to catch up to me.

Chapter Fifteen

Ryker:

Where the fuck could she be? I'd torn apart the area around the gas station searching for her, with no sign other than a recent shoe print that might not even be hers at the edge of the ferry landing. Why would Elena just take off like that?

I leaned against the fender of the Chevelle, trying to think. She left her bag, had no money, or anything, not even a jacket to turn the slight chill of the breeze off the River.

"The whole thing was my fault. I shouldn't have found a job or tried to leave. If I go back and do as he wants, he'll get his way. That's all he wants." Her words from earlier returned to haunt me.

She'd gone back, or tried to. Fuck!

I dragged my phone out of my pocket, trying to gauge how much time I wasted looking around here while Elena made her way back to a monster. "Hey, man, I got a problem." I explained to Stella what I suspected.

"A'ight, man, I'll head over to his place and watch for her. Call you when I got something." He ended the call.

A deep breath filled my chest and I nearly choked on it. This was not how it was supposed to go. For the first time in my life, I wanted to protect someone other than my Brothers, or my mom and sister. I wanted to make shit better for Elena. I didn't stop to examine the thought, only acknowledged it. Life sure as hell jumped up and grabbed what I wanted right out of my hands, though, just like always. Good to know some things never changed.

Well, I always worked my ass off for everything, so why

should Elena be any different? All I had to do was figure out how the fuck I was going to get her back and make her mine. I had no intention of letting life keep this particular prize from me.

I climbed in the Chevelle and cranked her up. Whatever way I found to get Elena back, I had to be where she was going so I could make it happen. For the first time since I got the car running, I didn't take a few seconds to just enjoy the rumble of the engine. The realization startled me as I put her in gear and eased out of the lot. Was I going to be one of those dickless bastards that gave up everything he loved just for a piece of ass? Not going to fucking happen. Elena was far more than just a chick to fuck, even though I refused to acknowledge it at the moment.

I took my time leaving town, winding through the side streets, just in case Elena hadn't managed to get far yet. No luck, though, so I headed on back up the River toward the bridge, taking my time. With any luck, I might find her walking along the road.

By the time I reached the bridge without Elena magically appearing on the roadside, I started to sweat. If she made it all the way back to Royse before I could get hold of her, things were going to be ten times worse that if she'd just done as she was told.

Royse's building sat right in the middle of the bad part of town, where historic buildings had been leveled to make room for high-rise low-income housing a few decades ago. All around it, a thriving community had boarded up and left for better places, leaving abandoned buildings and houses that had once been nice to fall into decay as poverty tightened its grip on the surroundings.

It all made the perfect storm for a monster like Royse. He came in and bought the last of the historic buildings just when a push came to save it from being torn down. Of course, the people who lived in the area didn't give a shit if the building fell in. The effort to save it came from the wealthy part of town, people who had the luxury of preserving good things from the past.

From the outside, at least, Royse had the building restored to its hey-day, and I heard no expense was spared to get the inside just as perfect. While he did it, he gave the neighborhood a hefty injection of money and hope, and for a little while, at least, things improved. A lot of folks depended on him for their daily bread during the restoration, and he found a way to keep some of them on after the work finished.

And in the process, he sunk his claws deep into every illegal thing that went on in the neighborhood. Not an eight-ball, rock, dime-bag, or anything else, sold without his blessing. Not a whore spread her legs without him getting his cut. He expanded from there until every illegal activity in the city and much of the surrounding area went through him.

For the first time, I wondered where the money for the restoration project came from initially. An average Joe didn't just wake up one day and decide to spend millions renovating a condemned hotel. I filed the thought away for future examination, if needed.

Unless I missed my guess, I needed to break Royse's stranglehold on southern Ohio to get Elena and her mom free, and that move wouldn't make me any friends in the local criminal community. They were happy to continue living on his dole, as long as it didn't cost them anything obvious.

As long as he remained untouchable, he would continue to threaten Elena, and me. Even though Elena thought her going back to him would fix everything, I knew better. I defied the motherfucker. He wasn't about to let that go. A man like him didn't make a rep on letting people get away with insulting him in his own damn house. At first glance, I thought his greed would be stronger than his need to make an example of me, but the more I considered it, the more I realized how that could have been a deadly mistake.

Taking the Chevelle through Royse's 'hood seemed like the mother of all bad fucking ideas, but I couldn't think of another choice right then. Time wasted on finding another ride might mean the difference between Elena alive and unharmed, and Elena dead, or worse.

I took a minute to stop and pull my little Smith & Wesson .40 out of the glove compartment and chambered a round. With the weapon riding all inconspicuous, tucked under my thigh for easy access, I pointed the car toward the bad side of town.

One of the few changes I made to the inside of the Chevelle during its restoration was a dash-mounted CD player, because at times, I refused to stomach any more classic country. For this little ride, Pantera seemed like a better choice than the Golden Oldies show. Didn't need a punk-ass thug thinking he could knock over some old fucker and grab a cherry car. So with *Walk* blasting through the open windows, I rolled slow down the street.

If Elena made it this far, she should have come this way. I needed to find someone to ask, and looking for trouble seemed the surest way of doing that. A slinger and his runners staked out a corner, but I passed them. She would avoid them, and they weren't likely to have noticed a non-buying bitch walking down the sidewalk.

In front of a boarded up business, I spotted a thin chick walking toward the next block, where the traffic was a little better. I slowed down even more and made a show of checking her out. Dark hair hung in a limp ponytail down her back, and a skimpy tank top framed thin shoulders. Her short shorts might have once been white, or even tan, but they had seen better days long ago.

The woman noticed me, and offered a smile before she

stepped off the curb. "Hey baby, you looking for some fun?" She leaned in the open passenger window as I stopped the car.

I pulled a fifty from my pocket and held it where she could see it clearly. "I'm looking for a friend of mine. Hot chick, early twenties, red hair. You seen her?"

Her smile faded. "Baby, I wish I could say yes. I need that money bad, but I ain't seen her. I been busy though. You might try El Chapo and his girls, two blocks down. They be out early." She moved to pull back.

I held the money out. "Thanks for being straight with me, sugar."

Her jaw dropped but she reached to take the money before I could change my mind. "Baby, you can ask me about your frien's any night. I'll even throw in a freebie for your fine self."

I couldn't help but smile. "Thanks, sugar. You have yourself a good night, okay?" As soon as she cleared the car, I let it roll again.

El Chapo, huh? Sounded like the kind of thug I normally went out of my way to avoid just to keep from killing them. And now I had to find one, and actually speak to him. Wonderful. Just fucking wonderful.

Traffic picked up a bit, most of it stemming from the drug trade, but some legitimate, too. A convenience store, which seemed to double as a grocery, had a steady stream of customers. Looked like mostly people walking to do their shopping. One woman, so heavy her many rolls flowed into one another, walked along, shepherding three kids ahead of her. All three carried several bags in each hand, while the woman kept her hands free to wield the long stick she used to keep the kids moving.

I shook my head with disgust and cruised on by. Bitches like that needed to be taught some respect for kids. That shit pissed me off like nothing else. At the moment, though, I had a bigger priority and no time for giving lessons.

On the next block, I watched for the pimp the girl called El Chapo. Surely, a punk who gave himself that name would stand out, even in a crowd. And he did.

The swagger gave him away first. Fucker walked like he had balls the size of milk jugs or something. I slowed down and when he came closer to a street light, what I saw left me completely unimpressed. Dirty blonde hair hit the tops of his shoulders, and a matching attempt at a goatee looked like something dead on his face. He kept tugging at pants with the waistband lower than his damn ass, and an oversized sports jersey hung loose halfway to his knees. Fake gold chains covered his thin chest like a suit of armor.

Two girls strolled along behind him, on the lookout for their next trick. Right away, El Chapo noticed my interest and nervously smoothed his goatee.

Good. I wanted the punk off balance. I stopped and lifted a hand to signal him to approach.

Boy followed orders real well. He came within a couple feet of my door. "Yo, man, you lookin' for somethin'?"

"Just information, my man. You got any of that?"

He shrugged and shifted from foot to foot. "El Chapo know ever'thing that go down in this 'hood, man." A nervous grin settled on his face. "Ever'thing got a price, you know what I mean?"

I grinned, the same one I gave an opponent in the cage right before I went for a takedown. "I got the price, if you got what I need."

He came in closer, still doing his anxious shuffle thing. "I gotta see the green up front, man, you know I mean? I don't front nobody nothin'."

I slid another fifty from my pocket and held it up. When he reached for the money, I pulled it back. "Not until I get the info, you know what I mean, my man? I don't let nobody fuck me over."

He paled a little. "A'ight, man, what you needin'?"

"I'm looking for a friend of mine. Cute chick, early twenties, red hair."

A speculative look crossed his face. "I might have seen somethin' like that."

I added another fifty. "I need to know when, where, and where she was going."

"I don't know, man. Talkin' out of turn is a good way to get dead, you know what I mean?" He started to step back.

"So is not holding up a deal. So you better start talking if you want to keep breathing."

He put his hands up. "Look, man, I ain' lookin' for no trouble. Bitch come struttin' up my street like she fuckin' own it, maybe twen'y minutes ago. I aks her who her daddy, and she say Royse. I let her pass, you know what I'm sayin'? Ain't no bitch worth dyin' over." He glanced around, as if he feared someone might rat him out to Royse. "That all I know."

I nodded, processing his words. "Okay, I'll let you off this time. If I find out you held out on me, I'll gut you like a Christmas pig. You know what I'm sayin'? Get it real clear, mother fucker." I held out the two fifties.

"I ain't messin' wit' you, man. I got a nice little gig going here, got my block, got my bitches, you know what I'm sayin'? I don't want no part o' no Royse shit."

I slapped the money in his hand and drove away. Shit. How the fuck had she made it there so quickly?

Chapter Sixteen

Elena:

After a couple of minutes, a second man came and led me through the lobby, and the soles of my new shoes squeaked on the marble floor. The place looked like some kind of fancy hotel from one of the old movies I sometimes had a chance to watch. Highly polished wood tables held big vases of fresh flowers under beautiful paintings. A few leather chairs were arranged in front of a huge fireplace covered by an ornate brass screen, and a polished wood counter stood to one side, as if waiting for guests to register.

I kept trying to swallow my fear, but it refused to stay down. The man led me down a broad corridor lined with huge paintings in gold frames alternating with heavy looking wooden doors. Near the end, he pointed me to a single wood chair against the wall.

"Wait here. I'll see if Mr. Royse has time to see you now." He tapped at the last door and went inside, closing it softly behind him.

With nothing to break up the silence in the hallway, I drummed my fingers restlessly on the arm of the chair. The sound echoed, drawing my attention upward. All my life, most of the buildings I'd been in had those stupid ceiling tiles that were supposed to muffle noise. This corridor had a high ceiling, with fancy swirls in the plaster, and elaborately carved moldings. Big chandeliers hung every so many feet.

The sense of stepping back in time almost made my skin crawl. I liked old buildings and historical stuff, but having it all look brand-spanking new? That was creepy as shit.

"Excuse me, Miss?"

Fuck, I hadn't even heard the door open. "Yes?" I jumped up. If my hands didn't have scorch marks, I'd be surprised.

"Mr. Royse is quite busy at the moment. I'll escort you to where you can wait for him." This guy seemed about as different from the first one at the door as my grocery list was from Ryker's.

I nodded, not trusting myself to speak after my stupid thoughts decided to remind me of Ryker at exactly the wrong moment. Thinking of him that way meant I had to do whatever it took to save him. I took a deep breath and followed the man, determined to go through with this.

We went back through the lobby and down another corridor, just as fancy as the first, but at the end, instead of another oversized painting, a set of double wooden doors that matched all the others I'd seen waited.

As we approached, the door swung open and a man who looked almost exactly like my escort waited. "Here we are, Miss. Mr. White will see you the rest of the way. Mr. Royse will come to you when he has a moment."

The new guy, Mr. White, held out a hand to invite me through the doors. I went, and waited for him. "This way, Miss."

Marble stairs led up several floors, with black wrought-iron railings. Another short flight of stairs went down, but they were regular concrete with a plain railing. And that's where Mr. White led.

"Where are we going?" My heart pounded harder as every movie I'd ever seen about the bad things that could happen in basements filtered through my brain all at once.

"Mr. Royse asked that you wait with your mother. Her room is this way." He stepped off the bottom step and turned to the left, hitting a light switch as he went.

Of course, I followed. This part of the building was entirely different from what I'd seen of the rest. Painted block walls led on forever, lit by big lightbulbs inside wire cages. Pipes of various sizes ran along the low ceiling. Every ten or twelve feet, there were big metal doors on both sides.

At the fourth set of doors, Mr. White stopped and pulled a huge bunch of keys from his belt and sorted through them until he found the one he wanted. He unlocked the door on the left, and held his hand out to gesture me forward.

I paused before going in the door, wary of what I might see. Rather than the gloomy dungeon I'd started to expect, the room before me looked like a cozy bedroom in a nice house might. I stepped through the door, only a little surprised when it immediately closed behind me.

Thick beige carpeting covered the floor, and the walls were off-white with pretty floral border and feminine pictures on the walls. A recliner waited to one side, some books on a table beside it. A big bed sat centered on one wall, covered with fluffy blankets and pillows.

Most important, my mom sat in the bed, leaning back against some pillows, and watching the huge TV mounted on the wall across from the bed. Her eyes shone with life like I hadn't seen in them for years, and her cheeks had some color. She hadn't seen me yet, giving me time to take it all in.

"Mom?"

She jumped a little, startled, then smiled broadly. "Elena, I'm so happy to see you! Mr. Royse said you would be here soon."

My thoughts derailed, and jumbled into one another. "H-he did?"

She nodded. "Come give me a hug. I can't believe you're finally here!" My mother hadn't shown that kind of emotion since…well, ever. At least, not that I remembered. The only feeling I could remember her expressing was hopelessness—not for our situation, but for her pain. She gave up long ago on ever finding freedom from it.

I went to her and wrapped my arms around her, careful not to hurt her. She returned the hug, squeezing hard, shocking me yet again. "Mom? What's happened?" Her wasted muscles and thin arms shouldn't be capable of that kind of strength. Hell, only a week ago, she could barely hold herself up long enough to shuffle the few feet to the bathroom.

"Oh, sweetie, when Mr. Royse's man came to the apartment and said he was there to bring me here, I was terrified, but he promised I would be okay. I saw a doctor, Elena, he came here!" Her face flushed with so much excitement my heart raced for her. "He ran some tests, but said he knew what was wrong with me! I'm on medicine now that helps, and I don't sleep all the time. I can't believe it, Elena! Your Mr. Royse has been so good to me."

Tears stung my eyes, and I didn't even react to the pronoun she put in front of Royse's name. She lived in a constant state of confusion, and I'd learned to just ignore little things like that. "I'm glad you're feeling better, mom." I came here expecting to find her dead, or at least worse than before. What the hell was I supposed to do now, knowing she was in the best shape she'd been in since she first got sick? I owed Royse. Any bargaining space I might have to protect Ryker just went up in smoke.

"Come sit with me and watch this show. I've found so many shows I didn't even know existed." Her attention went back to the TV and within seconds, it totally absorbed her again. At least that part hadn't changed. Just like a flick of a switch, the real world turned to nothing for her, same as always.

The damn tears refused to stay put, and spilled over my lashes. It was crazy, I'd shed more tears over the last few days than in my whole adult life. For the first time, I felt truly alive, and Ryker gave me that. Before him, I just went through the motions, trying to keep the body alive. My soul sat and waited in a hard little shell, and when I met Ryker, that shell cracked.

What the fuck was I going to do? Damn, I was so sick of that stupid question. Always before, I knew, because choices didn't exist. They still didn't, but I felt like they did. The whole situation screwed with my head. I took a deep breath and tried to clear my thoughts, getting nowhere fast. My heart and mind kept running back and forth, between my mom and Ryker, and finding no answers that saved them both.

After a while, I gave in to the exhaustion dragging at my muscles and slumped back against the pillows. I must have fallen asleep, because when I opened my eyes again, mom hadn't moved but a different show played. Mom's hand lay on one of the pillows beside me, and I reached for it, trying to clutch it and stay gentle at the same time.

She looked back at me with a smile. "Stop worrying, munchkin. It's going to be okay." The way she said it, then patted my hand just like when I was little, then went back to watching her show, tore my heart out.

How could I even question this? Royse had given my mother a new lease on life. I owed him. Nothing else mattered. Not me. Not Ryker. Not what Royse would ask in return. I would do it all, gladly, to give her life back to her.

Even with that realization, the memory of Ryker's gentle touch scalded my mind. How could I live and never experience that again? Or not see his smile, saying so much and showing so little? Ryker put everything I ever knew about men into doubt. He might be a fighter, but he'd shown me more tenderness than I could have imagined in the world. He took my problems on and helped me, even knowing the cost to himself. How could I just turn my back?

Tears rolled and still, I found no fucking answers. Why couldn't things be as simple as they had been a few weeks ago?

Back then, nothing mattered but surviving the day, and then the night, and then the next. I knew how to do that.

The door swung inward, silent. I might have missed it if I hadn't turned a little when I lay back on the pillows. My whole body locked in fear.

Royse stood there, a fake-as-shit smile plastered on his face. "Well, Elena, nice of you to join us. Your mom and I have been getting to know one another a little."

My mother stood—actually stood without wincing or groaning in pain—and went to him. "Mr. Royse, I'm so glad to see you." She went on tiptoe and kissed his cheek. "Thank you for bringing Elena."

Royse, entirely unlike the monster I knew him to be, kissed my mother's cheek and hugged her. "You're very welcome, Rosa. I know how much you missed your girl, and when she finished her work early, I asked her to go ahead and come to you." He led her back to the bed with a gentleness I couldn't believe he even possessed. "You rest, Rosa, and watch your show. Elena and I are going to talk for a few minutes."

I sat there in shock, unable to close my mouth, and looking like an idiot. Something was happening here, and I had no clue, but it scared the absolute piss out of me. An odd shaking started in my shoulders and traveled over my whole body.

"Elena, stop being rude, baby. Mr. Royse wants to talk to you." My mother hadn't scolded me in so long, I had no idea how to react. "Go on, now."

My body reacted automatically, following the command. I stood and went to Royse.

The look of victory in his eyes turned my stomach. The grin he gave me was the total opposite of the sweet smile for mom. "Good girl. Come on, let's go to your room and talk."

My room? What the fuck? The words refused to come out of my mouth, and I had to swallow and try again. "What are you doing here, Royse?"

He gave me that grin again, like a wolf watching a baby deer in the woods. "What am I doing? Elena, I'm just making sure my girlfriend's momma has the best care available. I couldn't very well let her sit there and suffer, now could I? Now come on, darling, let's go so you can tell me how your trip went." He put his arm around my waist and led me out of the room, closing the door behind him.

Chapter Seventeen

Ryker:

I really didn't want to believe it. Elena ditched my ass at a fucking gas station and made tracks back to her pimp as fast as she could go. What the fuck was I thinking, putting myself on the line for someone else? I fucking knew better.

I avoided this line of thought all the way here, until I knew for sure where she'd gone. Sure, it kept playing through the back of my mind, but I tried to ignore it, hoping she went somewhere else. No such fucking luck, though. Exactly the reason I never put my neck on the line for anyone except my Brothers. At least, I knew they wouldn't spit on the sacrifice like she had.

I pulled up by the boarded-up laundromat two buildings down from Royse's. Stella texted to meet him there when I checked in with him. And there he sat, that old beat-to-hell Honda of his smoking like a damn freight train.

"Man, why don't you shut that sonofabitch off, instead of sitting here pollutin' the air?"

He grinned and flipped ash from his cigarette. "If I shut her down, she probably won't start again without serious help."

I laughed, glad he didn't mind being ribbed about his ride. "She show up?"

He took another drag of his smoke. "Yeah, maybe fifteen minutes ago. Showed up, rang the bell, dude came and showed her in. Ain't seen nothin' since then."

"Well, shit." A few shots of JD would have tasted really good at the moment. Even though I knew where she went, the confirmation sent me reeling. I felt like I'd just been sucker punched. Figured. I let myself care a little for some chick, and she kicks me in the teeth. Story of my damn life. "Guess she didn't want help as bad as she thought she did, huh?"

Stella shook his head. "Nah, man, that girl was shaking so hard I could see it over here. She was terrified and thought she had no choice."

"I gave her a choice though, and fucked myself over doing it." Felt like the biggest fool in the fucking world. "I'm sorry to drag you into it. I'll get with Kellen in a couple days." I started the Chevelle, ready to get the fuck away from there.

"Hold up, man. She might have run back here, but li'l mama needs our help. You said Royse has her mom?"

The last thing I wanted to do was go back over it all, but Stella deserved to put his worries to rest. "Yeah. Guess he took the old lady from her apartment." The memory of her face when we ate flashed through my mind. "They had it really hard, man."

He nodded. "So she tried to get out and Royse grabbed her mom to keep her in line. Smart."

I had to admit, it was. "You think he hurt her mom when she ran?"

The thoughtful look on his face reminded me of the other Stella, the one who could run an international mob in his sleep. "I wouldn't. I'd keep the mom as a bargaining chip, and keep her in good shape."

"I guess that makes sense." I hated like hell to admit anything Royse did might have some kind of logic behind it.

"Did he contact her or anything?"

"I don't see how he could have. I was with her practically all the time, and I destroyed her cell phone." I searched my memory, looking for a time when she might have called someone, but came up empty. "Shit, I should have watched her closer. She thought if she came back, she could work shit out with him and keep him off my back."

"I can see that. She felt bad for getting you into it." He gave me a speculative look. "Ryker, I ain't gettin' in your business, but if you care anything for this girl, don't turn your back. The Brothers are all in. We'll help you get her out of there, and her moms too."

"I appreciate it, but she made up her mind. Best to let her ride it out." I swallowed back the sense of wrong the words caused. It didn't matter. She didn't want my help. All I could do was go back to my life and wish her well. "I'll catch you later, man. Got shit to do." I didn't, but at the moment, I sure as hell didn't want to sit there and talk about Elena with him.

"A'ight, man. Lemme know if you change your mind. Been a while since I kicked some scumbag ass."

I raised a hand and rolled away, headed back toward my place. The drive took forever, even though I only lived a few minutes away. Leaving Elena behind, forgetting about her, felt all kinds of wrong.

I glanced at my watch. One A.M. I had the key to Luke's gym. Pounding the fuck out of the heavy bag sounded like a great idea. With the Chevelle tucked safely into her spot in the parking garage, I headed up and changed, grabbed a bag, and got my blood flowing with a run to the gym.

The gym felt creepy without the lights and the sounds of training, and it smelled of antiseptic covering up stale sweat and blood. I locked the doors behind me, and turned on one bank of lights, just enough to see what I was doing. After a quick warm-up, I hit the bag, going at it hard with fists, knees, and then kicks.

Even after my muscles burned with exhaustion and trembled with the strain, I kept going. Yeah, stupid, and asking for an injury, especially since I hadn't been on my usual routine for a few days. But if I didn't get the anger and frustration out of my system, I would take someone's head off, or do something even more stupid. Like go into Royse's with guns blazing and take my woman back.

My woman. Where the fuck did *that* come from? Elena wasn't mine. Even if some part of me wanted her.

It was better this way, anyway. I had no time for a woman, between training and fighting and working my nine-to-five. Especially now that I'd lost the income from the underground fights. I'd always used that to fund my training. Now I would have to pick up extra shifts at work, until I figured out something else.

The line of thought made me angry all over again. I went out of my way for her, and she walked away without a backward glance, leaving me to deal with the consequences. How fucking stupid could I be? Life had kicked that lesson through my thick skull time and time again, and yet here I was.

Dripping sweat and ready to fall over with fatigue, I caught a quick shower, and headed back home. I needed some serious icing after that workout. And still, my brain kept feeding me bullshit about Elena, and how I was an idiot for turning my back. I reminded myself she turned away first. Her choice. Not mine. I just had to live with it.

By the time I made it to my building, I convinced myself all I had to do was get my ass back on track. Training and fight schedules kept playing on demand through my head. That little trick served me well every time I got too far up into my own head. Gradually, my focus and determination came back as I dragged my exhausted ass up the stairs.

And it all evaporated when I opened the door to my apartment and Elena's scent reached out to grab me. Fuck. My. Life.

I went in, closed and locked the door, and stood heaving against the wall. What the fuck? I made sure the fucking place was clean before we left, and she didn't wear strong perfume, so how could I still smell her here? Everything in me screamed at my stupid ass to go and get her. Except I couldn't. She wasn't mine, didn't want me. Nothing I could do about that shit.

About the only choice I had was to get my head tight, work, win fights, and get the fuck on with my life. Feeling pretty defeated, I headed for the couch, holding my breath and trying not to breathe her into my lungs. I dropped into my usual seat, and immediately, the memory of every fucking time she sat there flooded into my brain. Thoughts of the feel and taste of her followed hard, like a head kick.

I jumped up like the damn furniture burned me, my sore and aching muscles screaming at the abuse. Fuck. Epsom salt soak. That's what I needed. With a goal to work toward, I ran the water, dumped in the salt, and found something to read on the app on my phone. And when I climbed in to let the hot water and minerals work their magic, there she fucking was again, her memory taunting me.

Unable to keep my mind on reading, I settled for music and forced myself to stay in the tub for twenty minutes. When I climbed out, at least my muscles and joints felt a little better, even if the rest of me did feel like something the cat ate for breakfast and puked up for supper.

Exhaustion dragged my ass toward my bed as soon as I dried off. I pulled the blanket back and collapsed face-first, unable to roll over even when Elena's scent surrounded me stronger than ever. Fuck, I should have gone on to the clubhouse.

I drifted to sleep, too tired to fight off her memory, and not really wanting to, for that matter. There for just a minute, I had something real in my life, something outside the Hell Raiders. Some might argue fighting was real, and it was, of course, but it also reeked of fairy-tales. How many fucking kids had that dream? Plenty. Most worked a little, and gave up when it got hard. The few who stuck with the training made it a few fights, if they were lucky. Making it beyond the local gyms and clubs, though, and actually winning enough to have a chance at a title? Fucking fairy-tale. Pure and simple.

But Elena? She was real. So real, the dream reached out and grabbed me unexpectedly.

She sat on the ground, dirt smudged on her cheek as she cried and huddled over a lifeless form. I looked around, startled to find myself here. Dim light filtered into the alley from the street and a river rat the size of a big cat brazenly crossed the alley. Fucker didn't even care who saw him.

The rat went on about his business, and I moved closer to Elena, just watching her. I wanted like everything to reach out and take her into my arms, to help her, but my body refused to obey the commands. Instead, I stood frozen to the spot.

Her sobs increased and she tried to gather the body into her arms. "Mama, I'm so sorry. Forgive me. I swear I didn't know." She cried harder, and still I stayed still as a statue. Trembling, she started to rock back and forth. "Oh, God, Mama, I should have stayed with Ryker. He would have helped us." Her tears suddenly turned to screams of terror.

That fucking rat. The thing had grabbed her arm with its paws, pulling at her, claws breaking skin and making her bleed. It sat back on its haunches for a second and stared straight up at me, and I swear the fucker smiled. *A big, toothy rat smile. Then it turned back to Elena and opened its mouth. Long yellowed incisors flashed for an instant, right before they sank into her skin.*

Elena's screams of pain echoed in my ears as I jolted out of sleep, breathing like I just finished a marathon. The scene from the dream replayed in my head. Fucking crazy shit.

I forced myself out of the bed and went to the fridge for water and gulped down a whole glass. Going back to bed seemed like a stupid idea at the moment, but I still ached with fatigue. So, I reasoned with myself that the dream came from my worry over what Royse might have in store for Elena. And there was nothing I could do about that, right?

Chapter Eighteen

Elena:

As soon as the door closed, I pulled away from Royse's grip and spun on him. "What the hell are you doing?"

His lips pursed with disapproval. "I'm surprised at you, Elena. Come, let's talk in your room, where we won't be overheard." He glances significantly at the door separating us from my mom.

Everything in me said to run and never look back, but I couldn't do that, not when he had my mom. With no choice, I gave a tight nod and followed him.

Rather than open one of the doors in the basement like I expected, he led me back to the first floor and into the lobby. Beyond the counter, which still looked as if it were waiting for rich guests to sign in, he led me to an elevator with a beautiful brass-barred gate.

Proud as a damned peacock, he lifted the gate and followed me into the small space, closed it, and turned a dial next to the door. "When I bought this place, the old elevator shaft had been bricked up. I had it restored at great expense. It took months of research, poring through old newspapers and photographs, to get all the details exactly right."

I fought the urge to roll my eyes, careful not to piss him off any more than I already had. Did he really think I gave even one small fuck about his building? "It's very nice." I kept my voice neutral, neither encouraging him, nor telling him what I really thought.

The cab rose slowly with a sickening sway and mechanical noise that made me seriously doubt Royse's restoration job. If he paid someone to do it, they should be ashamed.

My nervousness must have showed as I clutched the brass handrail, because he smiled. "Don't worry, you'll get used to it. It's far more reliable than any other elevator in the city. No computer components to malfunction."

Get used to it? How many times did he think I would be in the fucking thing? A bell dinged and I jumped, startled. The needle on the floor indicator above the door hovered over the two. The machinery groaned some more and after a minute, the bell dinged again, as the needle switched to the three. Which floor was he taking me to?

The needle finally stopped at six, the highest number on the gauge. The elevator groaned to a stop and Royse raised the brass gate once more, gesturing for me to step out first.

I looked around, unsure what to expect. Royse took my elbow and guided me toward the far end of the corridor. "There are only two suites up here. Mine and yours. I kept everything to the same theme as downstairs, the same as the original hotel. The only difference is that, for the penthouse, everything is the best of the best available for the period."

My brain stayed stuck back there where he said *mine and yours.* Did he think I was here to play hotel, or house, or anything else, with him?

At the end of the hall, he turned to the left and opened a pair of heavy wooden doors, carved to match the engraving on the front door and everything else. Hesitant, I stepped into a marble floored entry and stared around me at the gleaming wood-paneled walls and shining brass coat racks and wall sconces.

The dim lighting gradually brightened, and Royse closed the doors. "I did have to concede to modern wiring, unfortunately. The original gaslights would have eventually ruined the art and the wood, even if they were practically smokeless."

I nodded as if I had any idea what he meant. He took my arm again and led me through an arch, into a room that looked like something out of both a magazine, and a history book. A black piano, the kind with the big wing raised to make it look like some kind of beast, stood before a big window.

Nearby, a beautifully carved bar sparkled with crystal glasses and bottles filled with rich-looking liquids. A pair of fancy sofas with delicate-looking striped upholstery faced one another over a bright Oriental rug. Everywhere I turned, some new beauty gripped me. Apparently, my wide-eyed silence pleased Royse.

"I'm so glad you like it, my dear. Now sit. Let me get you a drink." He waved me toward a pair of leather chairs facing a big fireplace like the one in the lobby.

Unsure what else to do, I sat and clenched my shaking hands in my lap. I had no clue what to do with this kind of crazy, so I just kept my mouth shut and waited to see what happened. Maybe, with a little luck, I might get out alive.

Royse approached with two glasses half filled with amber liquid and placed them on the little table between the chairs. He shrugged out of his suit jacket and tossed it negligently on the floor, loosened his tie, and sat and lifted his own glass.

"I apologize. I didn't know what you like, so I stocked my own favorites in the bar. I hope Lagavulin is acceptable."

Afraid of angering him, I took the glass and brought it to my lips. The strong liquor burned all the way down, but in a nice way. "This is good."

He sighed with what seemed like relief. "I'm so glad. I was worried." He took another sip from his glass. "Now, shall we get to business?"

"Please." I had no idea what else to say, and that seemed like a safer conversation than the La-la land he held me in from the moment he came into mom's room downstairs.

"You'll have to forgive me. I know this seems sudden, and I remind myself you had no idea of my feelings. Of course, if you had, you wouldn't have tried to leave me."

Whaaa…? My jaw dropped and I snapped my mouth closed. It seemed safer to stay silent, so that's what I did.

"But that's behind us now. You're back, and you won't try to leave me again. In fact, it's a good thing you forced my hand, and brought us out of the limbo we've been in since our first time together." He paused for another drink. "It brought me to my senses. I've been busy while you were away. First, I had your mother brought here and found her a doctor." He paused again, watching me.

"Thank you, she seems much better." What the fuck else could I say? The man had clearly lost his mind and instinct warned I had better play nice.

He smiled. "She was so happy to learn you and she would be living here with me from now on." The empty glass made a hollow sound as he set it back on the table. To my complete and utter confusion, he slid from his chair and got to one knee in front of me.

I drew back. This had gone entirely far enough. "Royse, I don't know what you want from me."

He held up a little black box with a smile. "Marry me, Elena. Be my queen. You'll never want for anything." He flipped the lid of the box back to reveal the biggest damn rock I'd ever seen on a ring. "Just say yes."

Oh FUCK! I was in big trouble. The funny part was, this little voice in my head screamed for me to say yes and take his ring. He might be a low-life crazy bastard, but he was offering me what every woman wanted—the fairy-tale ending.

My nerve endings jangled with warning. Piss him off and I would die in the next instant. I had to play along. "I…I don't know what to say. Royse, we don't even know each other."

This sappy grin plastered itself across his face. "I know everything I need to about you. Anything you'd like to know about me, just ask."

I drew a deep breath, trying to think how the heroine in some old movie might handle the situation. "This is a big step. Can I have some time to think?"

"Of course, my dear." He rose from the floor and put the ring box on the center of the mantle. "Take all the time you need. I can't say I'm not disappointed you didn't leap into my arms and scream yes, but I understand. This would mean a big change for you." He refilled his glass and sat once more.

I sat there, like a bump on a log, at a total loss for how to respond. The logical part of me wanted to insist he return to reality and tell me what the fuck he was trying to do. The little girl part of me nearly fell for his charade. And the smart part of me was scared to fucking death. This bastard had gone way off the deep end, and if I wasn't careful, he would drown me.

Ryker. I needed to get to Ryker. He would be able to help.

I stood. "I'm really tired. It's been a long evening. I should go home and get some rest."

Royse stood, too. "How inconsiderate of me. I should have realized, my dear. Of course, you're exhausted." He picked up his jacket. "You'll find everything you need, right through there. I'll be here at quarter of nine in the morning to take you down to breakfast."

My mouth threatened to fall open again. "I can't stay. I wouldn't want to be a burden." My mind scrambled to come up with something that wouldn't set him off. "Besides, I need to feed my cat."

A look of confusion crossed his face. "Your cat? You don't have a cat."

I thought fast, searching for a way out of the lie. "Well, no, not really. It's just a stray I feed, but it depends on me."

His expression cleared. "Oh, I understand. What does the cat look like?"

I shrug a little. "He's just a little tabby."

He nodded. "Okay. While you get settled here, I'll have someone go pick him up and bring him here to you." He smiled, pleased with his solution.

My heart pounded. I had to get out of here so I could go to Ryker for help. "He won't let anyone touch him but me. I'll have to go get him." There. That should do it.

He shook his head. "It's too late. I don't want you out at this hour. I'll send someone to put food out for him, then after breakfast, I'll take you to pick him up myself."

Fuck. If I argued the point any further, he would get suspicious and snap. "Okay, thank you."

He smiled and leaned in to kiss my cheek. "Have a lovely rest, my dear. I'll see you in the morning. You'll find clothing and everything in the dressing room."

He left and I collapsed back into the chair, shaking like a leaf. What. The. Fuck.

If anyone had ever suggested my life would take this kind of a turn, I would have laughed my ass off. This place, Royse… it was all like the fucking twilight zone. I kept expecting the creepy music to start.

No matter what, when he took me to get my imaginary cat, I had to find a way to get in touch with Ryker and let him know what was going on.

My stomach churned with horror. Except he wouldn't care. I'd ditched him at the first opportunity, and shoved his help away. But not until after I put him in danger. I was a fucking idiot.

Chapter Nineteen

Ryker:

I finally dragged my ass out of bed, feeling like I hadn't slept in days. A hot shower and some ice helped though. While I was doing all that, and eating breakfast, I refused to let my mind go to anything related to Elena. It took every ounce of the discipline I used in training and fighting, but I managed it. I even took the time to clean up after myself and get dressed.

The instant the .45 found its comfy spot in the holster inside the waist of my jeans, I grabbed my phone and hit Stella's number.

"Took your ass long enough, brother."

"You sound like you expected me to call, or something." Bastard knew me too damn well.

"Trying to figure out why you didn't call hours ago, motherfucker. What the hell's wrong with you?"

I shrugged and switched hands with the phone. "Dunno, guess I'm a dumb fuck, or something."

"First step to recovery is admitting there's a problem. Now, how we going to solve yours?"

We tossed ideas back and forth for a few minutes without coming up with anything groundbreaking. Finally, we decided to take another look at Royse's building. Maybe we'd find some secret there.

A half hour later, we sat in my Chevelle at the abandoned laundromat across the street, waiting as the city got on with its day. "You think she's still in there?" My mind raced with the possibilities. Royse could have killed her, or any number of other things by now. Why the hell had I been so stubborn?

Stella shrugged with his usual calm attitude. "No way of knowing for sure, unless we get someone inside, or we get eyes on her. For now, I guess we wait and see. I made a couple calls earlier, so maybe one of those ideas will pan out." He rolled his window down and lit a cigarette.

Any other time, I would bitch him out good for smoking in my car. At the moment, though, I didn't give a fuck. Way more important shit to consider.

Across the street, the blinds went up in one of the top floor windows, and a human form was briefly silhouetted against a light in the room, then disappeared. What could be on that floor? Living quarters, maybe? Offices? Fuck, for that matter, what did Royse even have in the building?

Stella's phone gave a soft ding, indicating an incoming text. He read and quickly tapped out a reply. "Okay, got a little info from my girl downtown. Royse bought this building for a song, when it was ready to be demolished, and set about restoring it. From what she can find, he returned it to very near original condition. It was a high-end hotel in the nineteen-twenties. He has it zoned as a single-occupancy home now."

Impatience beat against my chest. "What good does that do us?" Hell, I already knew parts of that.

"Not a lot, yet. But we do know he probably lives there. And we know the joint is important to him, or he wouldn't have put the money into it."

I nodded. "Okay, that makes sense. Still don't see how we can use that to get Elena back."

"Just hold on, brother. Matter of putting the little pieces together and getting the big picture. This is just the first corner. We'll get more, and soon."

Fuck, I wished I had Stella's certainty. I couldn't be so sure, though, with fear eating me from the inside out. What if my stubborn child bullshit had gotten Elena killed? Hell, I might never even know if she lived or died. My breath stuck in my throat, and I rolled the window down, trying to get some air.

"Hey, man, keep it together. We'll do everything we can to get her back." Stella gave my shoulder a slap that would have knocked me on my ass if I wasn't already sitting.

I nodded, more to convince myself than him. He could afford to sit there all calm and cool. His woman wasn't in the clutches of some asshole with delusions of grandeur, or whatever shit would cause him to dump millions into restoring a building like that. The thought clicked with something else in my head.

"Hey, Stella? What do we know about Royse's mental health?"

A cloud of smoke surrounded his head. "Not a great deal, why?"

"Just thinking. What kind of guy restores a building like that to the original condition unless he plans to make a lot more money off it than he puts in? Assuming he has no family ties to the building, anyway. I guess that would make a difference."

The cigarette butt went flying out the window. "I don't know, but we might be able to find out some stuff." He lit another smoke. "Now tell me what you're thinking."

I stared at Royse's building, putting it together out loud. "I'm not sure, but it seems to me the guy would have to be, I don't know, maybe obsessed with that period of history. The twenties was prohibition, gangsters, mob, all kinds of crime flourished. Underground fighting was a big thing. And prostitution. Bootleg booze. Guns. Street gangs. All of which we now know he's involved with. What if he imagines himself to be some modern-day Al Capone, or something?" I stopped and shook my head. "Never mind. It's too far-fetched."

Stella put a hand up. "Hold on. You might have something there. The fight posters. He has them printed to look like handbills from the twenties, or something. And the suits he wears all the time. I just figured he was too cheap to buy new, but they could be from that period, too." He nodded and pulled out his phone again, scrolled through his contacts, and sent off a long text.

"You got a way to find out?"

"Maybe. Got someone looking into it." Just like always, Stella kept his sources to himself.

I didn't mind, though, as long as it helped me get Elena back. Assuming she even wanted to come back to me, that is. What the fuck would I do if she didn't?

He nudged my arm. "Check that shit." He nodded to where a car pulled up in front of Royse's building.

I gave a low whistle. That was not just any car. A dark red 1930 Hudson Super Eight rolled to a stop, and a uniformed driver got out, spent a moment wiping the chrome of the headlamps. He stashed his rag, then opened the rear passenger door and stood waiting, hat in hand.

Stella and I slid down a little in our seats and kept watching. After a bit, the front door of the building opened, frosted glass and brass hardware gleaming, and a man in a black suit held it, also waiting.

A moment later, Royse came out with a woman on his arm. Her wide brimmed hat hid most of her face, but red hair showed clearly at her shoulders. She wore a pale-colored dress that dropped straight to her hips, concealing any hint of curves, then flared out a little and ended below her knees. Royse led her to the car, and she stopped for a second to take her hat off before climbing inside.

The flash of Elena's pale, terrified face sent my heart racing. Before I could straighten up and do anything about it, Royse got in after her and the car took off. I started the Chevelle and peeled out of the laundromat lot before it disappeared entirely.

I stayed back, trying not to alert the driver. When another car cut in front of me, I didn't push, just gladly used the buffer. Stella was on his phone, texting non-stop, but I didn't ask. I was too busy trying to keep my heart from jumping out of my chest.

At a four-way stop, a motorcycle idled, the driver busy with his cellphone, so he missed his turn to go. Royse's car went through, and the car behind him stopped. The bike turned and followed Royse.

"Okay, we can back off a little. That's our man on the bike."

Relief fought with my need to stop that Hudson, drag Elena out of it and kill Royse. The only thing truly stopping me was the knowledge that even if I took her back, we still had the issue of her mother. We had no idea where Royse had her, or if she was even still alive. So I hung back and bided my time.

That old car created quite a stir, driving through a rough part of town. The few people out so early stopped and gawked. The bike stopped at a shop, one of the few we'd seen still open, and an old beater car came out and took his place. I edged a little closer, but still didn't push. If Royse or his driver made us, Elena would be in more danger than she already was.

When Royse's car pulled over in front of a rundown apartment building, Stella's buddy in the beater went on by, and so did I, careful not to pay too much attention. I took the next right and parked next to a burned out church.

I didn't even have to ask. Stella got out and walked back toward where Royse had parked. I practically held my breath, staring at my phone, willing it to give me some kind of update. A smoke would have been good right about then, even if I didn't smoke. Anything to pass the fucking time.

After half an hour and no word, I gave up and went to the trunk to dig out an old baseball cap. With the hat pulled low, I strolled in the direction Stella had disappeared. He was nowhere in sight when I rounded the corner, so I kept walking.

Shrill sounds and shouted curses caught my attention, just in time to see Royse stumble from the alley beside the apartment building. He held something small and furious at arm's length, shouting directions to his driver.

The man hurried and dragged one of those plastic pet carrier crates from the back of the car and held it open. Royse tried and tried to thrust the squirming thing in his grip into the carrier, but it resisted strongly.

I got a little closer and just stopped, shaking my head. The fucker was trying to put a screeching, scratching, biting cat into the carrier, and it clearly had other ideas. Surely he hadn't just grabbed up some stray alley cat?

Stella crossed the street and approached Royse, speaking quietly, then helped him get the cat inside the crate and the door closed. Royse stood there, cursing and wiping blood, and occasionally replying to whatever Stella said.

After a moment, Stella laughed a little, leaned down to peer into the car and said something, then walked away with a half salute. I stepped behind the corner of a building, and waited. Stella gave me a slight nod as he passed without breaking stride, and I stayed put.

Royse's car went by, slow enough for me to get a good look at Elena's face. She wore a smile, but looked even more frightened than before. As soon as it was out of sight, I jogged back for the car to see what Stella had learned. I couldn't wait to hear what would make a bastard like Royse pick up a feral cat and try to rescue it. Didn't they usually use traps for that kind of thing?

Chapter Twenty

Elena:

I finally managed to breathe a little as the driver pulled away from my building. The whole time Royse was trying to catch an alley cat, I just knew he was going to kill me for mentioning a cat. He refused to let me out of the car to help, or I could have just pretended to give up.

And then I saw Juaquin watching from the stairwell door. He recognized me, and started toward the car with a big grin. Thank God he saw me shaking my head and went back before Royse spotted him. Those two meeting would not go well.

When Ryker's friend, Stella, came over and helped get the damn cat in the cage, I thought I would die. But Royse climbed in the car after Stella leaned down to wave at me, and we left. I nearly choked to keep from laughing at all the blood dripping from Royse's hands. I had to look away.

Ryker. Right there in plain sight. My stomach threatened to get rid of the fancy breakfast Royse made me eat. If he got caught, we would both die. I found that out earlier when one of Royse's men came in during the breakfast thing, and reported they still hadn't found Ryker. One of the fancy china plates flew against the wall, shattering, as Royse screamed for them to bring him Ryker's head. The entire morning left me even more terrified of Royse than before.

Behind the seat, the cat yowled and hissed, pitching a fit about everything. Royse leaned to look at it, still trying to stop the bleeding from his bites and scratches. "My dear, I do hope this cat settles down. I would hate to have to kill it."

My stomach did the threatening thing again. I couldn't let him kill the poor thing. "I told you, he doesn't like people. We should have just left him there, where he's used to being. I could ask the neighbor to put food out." My heart pounded in fear of his reaction.

So far, Royse hadn't showed any signs of violence against me, but that didn't mean shit. He nodded, calm as could be. "Yes, my dear, we probably should have. But I want you to be happy in your new home. If a stray cat helps, then you'll have your cat."

I swallowed hard. "I don't need a cat to be happy."

He brushed one finger over my cheek, with a sappy-ass smile that said he'd gone completely around the bend. "I'm glad to hear that, darling. I feared the transition might be difficult for you." His fingers snapped, getting the driver's attention right away.

"Yes, sir?"

"Go back where we were. My fiancé has decided we don't need the cat."

Fiancé? I fought back a gag. Shit, I had to find some way out of this mess. At least, it seemed like Ryker and Stella might be willing to help. I felt like the biggest fool in the world for leaving Ryker like that. He'd been nothing but good to me, and I shoved it back in his face. Stupid.

Of course, that was just normal for me. Give me two bad choices, and I would take the worst one, every damn time. The driver stopped in front of my building again, breaking my train of thought. Panic surged. I had to find a way.

"Wait!" I laid a hand on Royse's arm before he climbed out. "I'd really like to let the cat go. Would that be okay? So I can say goodbye?" I kept my voice low and gentle, trying to be the woman he seemed to want me to be.

"Of course, darling, if that's what you want. Come, I'll walk with you." He got out and held his hand to help me. My skin crawled at the thought of touching him again, but I had no choice. He brought the cat cage and kept his other hand at the small of my back, guiding me into the alley.

I made a big show of leaning down to baby-talk the hissing, spitting cat like it was one of those spoiled rich-people pets. Oddly enough, it calmed a little at the sound of my voice. I managed to open the cage without getting bitten or scratched, and the poor cat darted out of the cage. He disappeared under the dumpster before someone could grab him again. Poor thing would probably have nightmares about being cat-napped for weeks.

The thought made me smile a little, and before I could move away, Royse wrapped an arm around my shoulders and kissed my forehead. "It's so good to see you happy, darling." The man had definitely lost a few marbles or something, to go from trying to have a trick kill me to treating me like a princess or something.

Fear scooted over my skin at how easy it would be to tip him back in the other direction. The wrong word at the wrong time, and the switch would flip. If that happened, he would kill me himself. I had to be very careful what I said and did, and still find a way to contact Ryker.

"Thank you for taking care of me." I leaned into his side, hoping he would take that as a sign of affection. "Is it okay if I talk to my old neighbor and ask him to put food out for the cat?"

He squeezed me a little. "Of course, darling. Let's go." And just like that, he led me back to the front of the building and up to the door.

Now what the hell was I supposed to do? I hadn't dared to hope he might actually let me speak to Juaquin myself. At best, I thought he might have the driver pass along a message. But no, it seemed I would at least get to see Juaquin myself, even if Royse did the talking. He led the way into the stairwell, keeping a firm grip of my arm.

Juaquin appeared at the top of the six steps that led up to the first floor, a gun held down next to his leg. "What can I do for you folks?" There was no mistaking the hostility in his voice. He acted like he didn't recognize me. My drug dealer neighbor suddenly frightened me far less than the man at my side.

"Juaquin, it's Elena." Speaking first, without Royse's permission, seemed like a big risk, but I took it anyway. Getting hit by a stray bullet wasn't high on my list of things to do.

A broad grin settled on Juaquin's face. "Well, look at you, girl. Look like you done foun' Prince Charmin'. How you momma doin'?"

I forced a smile. "She's real good." I patted Royse's arm like a proud girlfriend or some shit, trying to figure out how to word things to give him the information I needed passed to Ryker. "Royse got her a doctor and everything. She even has a room of her own in his building."

Juaquin's eyebrows rose. "I'm glad to hear it. So that's where you stayin' at now?"

Royse cleared his throat as I nodded. "Oh, yeah, could you feed that little alley cat I was feeding for me? And if my friend Stella from the library comes around asking for me, just tell her mom's doing great and I'll see her as soon as I get settled." Hopefully, Juaquin would connect the dots and if Stella, or Ryker, came asking for me, would give them the message. I couldn't chance saying anything more direct.

Juaquin nodded, but his eyes narrowed a little. "Stella, huh? Remind me which one she is. You know I don't pay no 'ttention to names."

I widened my eyes and gave a fake giggle. "You know, the one that looks like a dude in a leather skirt. Little too much facial hair."

"Oh, yeah, I 'member that chick." He adjusted his shirt. "Not my type, but she smokin'."

"That's her. Thanks Juaquin, I owe you one."

Royse cut my reply short with a tug to my arm. "We should go, darling."

"Of course." I turned back toward the door.

"Hey, Elena."

I looked over my shoulder to see what Juaquin wanted.

"You don't owe me nothin', girl. I'll let your friend know. You just take care yourse'f, hear me?" His big smile nearly made me miss the deadly serious glint in his dark eyes. It looked like my whole act hadn't fooled him one bit.

"I hear you. I'll do my best." Before I had a chance to say any more, Royse led me back outside and to the car. Not long after, the driver stopped us in front of Royse's building, exactly where he first picked us up.

Royse told the driver to wait, and helped me out of the car and to the door. A man who looked exactly like the ones from last night met us there. "Take my fiancé to her suite, Green." He leaned in to kiss my cheek. "I'll be back in time for dinner, darling. Green here will help you if you need or want anything." And just like that, he went back to the car, leaving me alone.

Not sure what else to do, I followed Green inside to the elevator. The only thing I wanted to do was run to the basement and grab mom, and get us both the hell out of there. Even if I could get to her, though, she wouldn't be willing to go with me. She'd fallen hook, line, and sinker for Royse's craziness.

Riding up in the elevator, I tried to think back to the last real conversation I had with my mom before yesterday. For so many years, she'd been locked inside her own head, as if to escape the pain of her disease. It had been a long time since she and I had talked about anything more than my trying to convince her to eat. She had sometimes asked how my day had gone, but I lied, knowing she didn't really want the details.

Green opened the elevator gate about the time I started

wondering if my mother even cared to know the truth about Royse and what was going on here. After all, he helped her to not have so much pain, and made her comfortable. With what she'd gone through, would anything else matter to her? Should it matter to me?

At the door to my rooms, I turned back to Green. "Do you think it would be okay if I went downstairs and had lunch with my mom?"

I held my breath while he appeared to consider. Finally, he nodded. "She has lunch at one. I'll come back up and escort you to her."

"Thank you." I hid my sigh of relief and slipped inside the big carved door.

Fear had kept me from exploring too much last night and this morning. I didn't think Royse would be too happy with me looking for weapons or a way out of his beautiful bird cage. With him at least out of the building, I might not get a better chance.

I started looking around carefully, worried Royse could have cameras in the rooms. I tried to make sure I just looked curious about my new home. Time got away from me as I checked out all the luxuries I'd only ever read about or seen in movies.

It seemed like just a few minutes had passed when Green knocked on the door and asked if I was ready to go to my mom. The temptation to fake a headache and keep exploring was hard to resist, but I also needed to find out more about my mom. It came as a shock that I knew so little about her, beyond her health shit. Hell, I had no idea if she would even really object to my being a whore to support us. I always just assumed she wouldn't like it.

Chapter Twenty-One

Ryker:

I slid into the driver's seat, once more not saying a word about Stella's smoke. "What was that all about?"

He exhaled a cloud of smoke on a half laugh. "Apparently, Mr. Royse's lovely fiancé missed her cat."

"What?"

"Fucker is completely off his rocker, man. He's calling your girl his fiancé and she's all frantic, shaking her head behind his back. Looked scared out of her wits."

"So, what, he went and got her a feral alley cat?" I didn't know whether to laugh or be furious.

Stella gave a full laugh. "He said she just moved to her new apartment, on the penthouse floor of his building, but it was a big change. Apparently that run-down shit-hole was where she lived before. He made a joke out of her being barely able to feed herself, and still she fed some stray cat on the street."

"He's bringing the cat back to his building?"

"So it seems. Wants her to be comfortable." Stella paused to shake his head and flip ashes out the window. "I have serious doubts about that cat, though. If a human ever bothered to feed it, especially on a regular basis, it shouldn't be so skinny. And the way it acted, no human ever touched it, either."

I sat there for a long moment, absorbing what he said and thinking about it. "You think she found a reason to come back to her place?"

He nodded. "I just can't figure out why. She didn't even get out of the car."

I started the car and pulled out, heading back past Elena's building. Shock almost made me stall the Chevelle when I spotted Royse's antique car sitting there again, in the same spot. But what surprised me more was the sight of Elena on Royse's arm, coming out of the alley. Royse carried the empty cat cage in his other hand, and kept smiling down at her.

Every instinct demanded I stop and grab her away from Royse, rescue her, but I forced myself to drive on by. Going as slow as possible without making the whole damn street suspicious, I watched in the rearview as Royse led her up the steps to the front of the building.

"Hang a left here."

I followed Stella's direction without asking why. All I needed to know was that he had a reason, or he wouldn't have said it.

"Pull over here and wait." He hopped out and strolled back to the corner, where he leaned casually against a wall. He looked directly toward Elena's building, not bothering to stay out of sight.

I slid down in my seat and watched in the side mirror as my Brother hid in plain sight. No matter how much I wanted to yell at him to make sure Royse didn't see him, I knew he was right. The easiest way to make someone suspicious, or make them think they were being watched, was by skulking around and trying not to be seen yourself. So I waited.

Less than ten minutes, and he headed back to the car. "Okay, they left again." He got in. "Let's get out of here for a bit, then come back. We need a less conspicuous ride."

Anxiety rolled my gut all over the place as I drove back to Stella's place. "Tell me again why I shouldn't just turn around, force Royse's car over, and take Elena from him?"

Stella sighed. "Wish it was that simple. She went back to him thinking she could protect you, and to find her mom. If she ain't found what she's looking for yet, she probably wouldn't leave with you."

"I could make her, though." Stubborn desire to do exactly that refused to be silent.

"You could." He nodded. "But if she doesn't know where her mom is yet, how long before she ditches you again and goes back?"

I brought my hand down hard on the steering wheel. As bad as I hated to admit it, the fucker was totally right. "So what do we do?" I pulled into a parking place next to his old beater.

"We go back to her building, see what she did while she was there. Maybe she talked to somebody. Or maybe we can find somebody with more information, at least." He got out, then leaned back in the window, tossing me a set of keys. "Here, move any firepower you have over to my ride. I'm going to grab us a few things, just in case an opportunity comes along."

I didn't keep many weapons in the Chevelle. The thing drew attention from every damn cop that spotted it, and I'd rather not get pulled over with a trunk full of illegal guns and ammo. Still, I had no intention of needing a firearm and not having one. I climbed out and grabbed a few spares from the hidden compartment I'd built under the rear seat.

By the time Stella got back with a heavy looking gym bag, I had climbed in his car and checked over all my weapons. He laughed a little as he got in the driver's seat. "Figured you had some hardware along for the ride."

I shrugged a little. "Yeah, just not much. Rather not have some trooper with an eye for muscle cars pull me over just to admire my wheels, then find a bunch of guns in it."

Stella laughed again. "Yeah, man, that'd be just about your luck." He coaxed his old beater into starting up, and we started back for Elena's place.

We didn't talk during the drive. For one thing, I was too keyed up to bother with conversation. Stella seemed unusually edgy, too. Nothing ever rattled him, but he drummed his fingers on the steering wheel as he drove. That by itself told me he wasn't his usual laid-back self.

Royse's car had disappeared when we drove back past Elena's place. I had to push back the feeling of failure and disappointment trying to settle on my shoulders. Allowing Royse to take her somewhere else went against everything my mind said about the situation.

Stella went around the corner and parked in the same space I did earlier. "Let's go see why they came back here."

During the walk to the apartment building, I felt like a kid on the way to the principal's office. Dread filled me at what we might find out. I didn't have to wait long, though. As soon as we started up the steps, the front door opened.

A tall, thin black man, probably about my age, stayed inside. "One o' you happen to be called Stella, get on in here."

Stella and I exchanged a look, then went inside. The guy led the way to a first floor apartment and motioned us inside. It made me nervous as fuck, but I went in, after a pause to make sure my .45 sat easy in the holster and ready. Inside the dimly lit apartment, we stood and waited while the guy checked up the stairwell, then closed the door.

He gestured for us to follow, and led the way into a kitchen that looked like a cross between a chemist's lab and some old granny's kitchen. "Which one o' you be called Stella?"

"That's me. You mind explaining how you know my name?" The scowl on Stella's face should have scared the guy to death. Seemed like Stella might have lost his touch.

The man grinned with a flash of gold teeth. "Got my ways. Ya'll know my girl, Elena?"

Holding back my growl of frustration sent my stomach rolling again. "Yeah, we do, and you got about three seconds to start talking."

"I gotta make sure ya'll the right ones before I can say

anything." Bastard sounded stubborn as a mule.

The growl got away from me. "Look, man, she's in big trouble, and her mom is, too. Royse is dangerous as fuck. We ain't got time for this bullshit."

"I'm Juaquin, and I kep' an eye out for her last couple years. She looked good when she was here earlier, all dressed up and ridin' in a sharp car. How I know you ain't the trouble lookin' for her?" The guy's glare cut from me to Stella and back again.

The deep breath I took did absolutely no good. I explained as quickly as I could. "If you know something that could help her, we need to know now."

Juaquin nodded. "A'ight, I guess. Man scared the fuck out o' one o' my runners, back there prowlin' in the alley for a damn cat. After he caught it, they left in his fancy car, but came back a few minutes after and let the cat go. Came as a real shock to me when she came up lookin' so different." He repeated the conversation he'd had with Elena.

Stella listened carefully. "Well, at least we know she's okay and he ain't turning her out right now. And we know he didn't kill her mom."

"True, but that don't mean I have to like it." My jaw clenched until I thought my molars would crack under the pressure. "And we're no closer to getting her back."

Juaquin went to the stove and pulled something from the oven. "Ya'll want some stuffed peppers? I got plenty."

My stomach rumbled loudly. "Thanks, man, but we don't have the time."

He shrugged. "Suit yourself. I got more to tell you, though, but you don't seem interested. Your loss." Within a couple minutes, he had found a plate and started piling it high.

Stella grabbed himself a plate and followed suit, leaving me no choice but to do the same. "What else you got?"

"You ever see the inside of Royse's building?" Juaquin

went to the living room and dropped into a chair, gesturing for us to do the same.

I shook my head. "No, never been in it. Why?" Flavor exploded across my tongue with the first bite, reminding me stuffed peppers were definitely not on my food list. Fuck the damn food and training for the moment. I could get back on track when I had my woman back. This time, I didn't even resist the thought. I could work that shit out later, too.

"I'm a business man. I make a habit of keeping tabs on my competition. Shorty down at the courthouse got me copies of the floor plans for the renovation." Juaquin paused for another bite. "Anyways, if you plan on taking that fucker down, I want in."

That statement put me on edge. "Why would we let you in? We don't know you from fucking Adam."

"You got any other way of getting' a look inside that building without walking through the door?"

He had a point. Information about Royse's building would help. "Why you want in? Wouldn't it make more sense for you to lay low and not let him notice you? Then when he's gone, just move in and take over his territory?"

He nodded around another bite. "I was fine with that until a few days ago. Fucker killed my lookout, who also happened to be my cousin. I want a piece of Royse's hide."

I glanced at Stella. His almost imperceptible nod showed his agreement. We needed the damn floor plans that bad. "Okay, but you remember this is our operation. You do exactly as we say, when we say it. Understood?" Fuck, I hated bringing in somebody we didn't know. No way around it this time, though. I would just keep a close eye on him, and blow a hole through his skull at the first sign of a double-cross.

Juaquin shrugged. "Fine with me." He worked his way through the rest of the food on his plate.

Chapter Twenty-Two

Elena:

Being led down to my mom's room for lunch creeped me out. Mr. Green was as nice as the other people who worked for Royse seemed to be, but the whole thing just seemed weird, on an epic level. I knew better than object or say what I thought, though. People around Royse who did that ended up beat half to death, or just dead. I'd both seen, and heard, it too many times to count. Keeping my mouth shut seemed like the best option.

Praying wasn't my thing, but I offered up a few words to ask that Ryker and Stella got my message through Juaquin. If they didn't bother, I was fucked. Nobody would rescue me, and I would have to live with whatever kind of crazy Royse planned. That thought made my stomach burn, a feeling I was getting used to lately.

Mr. Green opened mom's door for me, and I tapped at the door before I went in. "Hi, Mom, how're you feeling?"

She looked up from where she sat in the big plush recliner. "Hi, sweetie. I'm glad you came." A smile curved her lips, but didn't reach her eyes.

I ignored warning bells going off in my head. "I thought I'd have lunch with you, if that's okay."

She nodded. "It'll be here in a few minutes. I asked them to hold it for a half hour so we could talk."

My eyebrow went up. "That sounds serious."

"Well, it is." She straightened the throw covering her legs. "Mr. Royse came in a while ago."

"Oh? And what did he want?" My pulse raced. Why the hell did my mom want to talk about Royse?

Her graying hair curled over her shoulder as she shook her head. "He stops in to check on me every day. He was very upset today." One hand came up as if to silence me. "Why in the world did you tell him you had a cat?"

Anger raced through me, and my face went red-hot. "What?" I took a breath. "Mom, what would you know about a cat? You were always asleep or just zoned out, or whatever. You barely noticed if I was even there. So, yeah, I had a cat. At least I could talk to him sometimes and know he heard." Wherever all that bitterness and anger came from, there was still plenty more, but I managed to plug the leak. And part of me couldn't help wishing I really *did* have that fictional pet. Someone would have known I was alive, anyway, and cared, even if only that I came with the food on time.

Her brows went down in a frown. "Don't talk to me like that, young lady."

I took a deep breath and tried to keep a handle on my temper. "I'm not being disrespectful, Mom. Just stating a fact."

Her face flushed, and my mind went back to my childhood, bringing back details I had chosen to ignore the last several years. She pointed at me. "You listen. I nearly worked myself to death trying to take care of you. I won't have you speak that way. And to be so mean to Mr. Royse? What happened to the girl I raised?"

I couldn't help it. The bitter laugh escaped and my self-control snapped. "Mean? The girl you raised? I don't know, Mom. I haven't seen that girl in so long I don't even remember her. What I do remember is having to beg strangers for help. And when that failed, I remember your kind Mr. Royse raping me, then turning my ass out. That's how we had a roof over our heads, even if it was a shitty one, and food in our bellies." I stood up. "I've lost my appetite."

Mr. Green had left the door unlocked when he left, so I slammed through it and practically ran down the hall and back up to the lobby. When I got to the elevator, I realized I wasn't sure how to make it work. Rather than wait around, though, I turned the dial and hoped for the best.

Back inside my suite, I sat on the fancy sofa and seethed with fury. What had that been about? Angry tears rolled down my cheeks as I replayed my mother's words. It occurred to me Royse had decided to use her as a weapon. Instead of threatening to not help her, he could easily still be the good guy if he convinced her I was ungrateful or disrespectful.

A soft knock at the door interrupted my thoughts. "Miss? Are you okay?"

I hurried to wipe the tears away and stood to face Mr. Green. "I'm fine. I'm sorry, you weren't anywhere in sight, and I was in a hurry, so I just came back up on my own." The smile I gave him was shaky, but it was the best I could manage right then.

"Apologies, Miss. Next time, I'll wait outside the door for you."

"No need. I'm sure it won't happen again."

He nodded and left, closing the door softly behind him.

I sat for a minute, trying to calm myself a little, but with no luck. I was glad my mom had less pain now, but I couldn't forgive her for what our survival cost me. How could she act as if none of that mattered? Tears stung my eyes and no matter how hard I blinked, they refused to stop. A sudden sob gripped my chest, and I slipped to the floor and gave in. Time meant nothing while I cried my heart out, grieving for what should have been.

"Miss? Are you okay? I knocked, but you didn't answer." Mr. Green came close. "Miss?"

I tried to wipe my tears and get control of myself, but the harder I tried, the harder I cried. A gentle hand touched my shoulder, and like an idiot, I practically climbed up the poor man so I could cry all over his nice suit.

After a minute, he wrapped his thin arms around me and made soothing noises, and held me for the longest time, until I wore myself out. "I'm so sorry." The crying had faded to hiccups, and shame set in. "I've ruined your jacket."

"Don't worry about it, Miss. My wife and daughter have done the same, more than a few times." He gave a soft chuckle. "Something you want to talk about?"

Yes, I did, but I couldn't say too much. I shook my head. "Just my mom. I gave up everything to take care of us while she was sick, and now she acts like it was nothing."

He was quiet for a minute. "Can I ask you something?"

"Sure." I braced myself, fearing what he might ask.

"You don't want to be here, do you?"

Startled, I looked up into kind blue eyes. "No, I don't. But Royse brought my mom here, took care of her, made her better. I don't have a choice. And now, after everything he did to me, he acts like I'm his girlfriend."

Mr. Green nodded. "I thought as much." He looked around, as if worried someone might hear. "You have someone else?"

Did I? It hit me all of a sudden. I wanted way more from Ryker than a rescue. I wanted a future with him. "Yeah, I do. He tried to help me get away, but I came back because of my mom. He probably doesn't want anything to do with me now."

Another knowing nod. "He drives a black sports car?"

My heart bruised my ribs. "Yeah." How could he know?

"He was watching the building. Be ready when he comes back."

"What?" My mind raced.

He lowered his voice to a whisper. "Be ready. He'll come for you. I'll help however I possibly can."

The tears threatened to come again. "I... I can't leave. My mom—"

"Will be fine. If he can't use her for leverage, he'll order her killed. But don't worry, none of us here would kill a defenseless sick woman. We'll make sure she gets out." His words refused to sink in.

My head spun. Could any of this be possible? Or just a trap? "But I've seen what happens when he orders somebody punished. His men like it."

He nodded again. "They don't work here. They're involved with his illegal businesses. The rest of us aren't like that. They come and go here, because he has various offices in the building, but usually, it's just the staff—a chef and kitchen help, housekeeping, and an attendant for each floor."

All of this seemed so strange, completely at odds to what I knew about Royse. "So, I could just leave?"

"Oh, no, it isn't that simple. The security man, the one who usually is in the lobby, won't let you just leave."

My heart sank a little with disappointment. I nodded. "I understand."

"Good. Now, since you missed lunch with your mother, I brought you a tray. You should eat, and keep your strength up." He patted my shoulder and left with hardly a sound.

I decided to take his advice, and found the tray on the small table in the entry. I brought it into the room I'd come to think of the as the living room, to an oval table with four chairs by the windows. When I took the cover off the tray, I just stared for a minute, stunned. Instead of the sandwich I sort of expected, a grilled chicken breast sat atop what looked like rice. Little green balls, which I suspected were Brussels sprouts, lay to one side on the plate. A small bowl held a fresh salad, and another plate was covered with fancy crackers with thin slices of cheese and meat.

There was enough food on that tray to last me a week. I took a couple of bites of everything but the Brussels sprouts. Those things just didn't look as if they were meant to be eaten. It all tasted delicious, but there was no way I could eat it all. I put the cover back on the tray, unsure what I should do with it.

Exhaustion won out, and I left the tray where it was, and went to the soft bed in the bedroom. Someone had been in while I was out with Royse, and made the bed even though I left the blankets straightened when I got up. I felt guilty for undoing the work by pulling the blankets back, but tiredness forced the issue.

Sleep took over as soon as my cheek touched the pillow. Screwed up dreams made me toss and turn while Royse and his henchmen chased me through my sleep. I woke breathing hard and calling out for Ryker.

Chapter Twenty-Three

Ryker:

It took more time than I wanted it to. My instincts kept insisting I should just go to Royse's building and walk in with guns blazing and take Elena back. Every time I put that suggestion up, Stella shot it down fast, saying we needed a plan that included her mother. I got that, but at the moment, I didn't give a shit about the old lady. I just wanted my woman safe and sound in my arms.

By this point, I wasn't fighting it. Elena was my woman, and I had every intention of telling her exactly that, as soon as I had her back. We would deal with the details once she was safe again.

"Hey, Ryker, since you're not adding to this discussion, how about you call the boss and give him an update? Better than you sitting here looking like somebody kicked your dog." Stella's words came with a grin, but it meant he was worried.

I stood. "Yeah, probably a good idea." I slid my phone out of my pocket and headed for the door. I'd rather take my chances with being overheard on the street than counting on a drug dealer not to have his place wired. The sidewalk seemed like a far safer bet.

Kellen came on the line, and I filled him in as I walked up and down the sidewalk to make a more difficult target for anyone listening or taking aim at my skull.

"Okay, got a time frame yet?" The wheels turning in Kellen's head practically made my phone rattle.

"Not yet, but the sooner the better. Can't be soon enough for me."

"I heard that. A'ight, I'll send some boys your way. You might need backup." He went silent for a minute. "Ryker, she'll be okay, man. You have to believe that."

Frustration flared up, but I bit back the words on the tip of my tongue. Kellen went through hell with Vicki when they first got together, so he had a real good idea how I felt. "Yeah, trying to stay positive."

"Good. Okay, keep in touch. Sending the boys to Stella's place when they hit town, but they have your number, too. They'll holler at you before they get there." He ended the call and I headed back inside.

Stella and Juaquin had a bunch of papers spread over the table and were leaned over, studying them closely, and talking quietly. I moved closer for a better look, more than a little shocked to see a pencil drawing of the front of Royse's building at one end of the table. I bent over to see what they were talking about.

"This right here don't make sense. If he lives on the penthouse floor, why have two apartments up there?" Stella traced his fingers over what looked like a mirror image floor plan on each side of the building. "Think he has any relatives or anyone else living there with him?" He glanced up at me, like I might know.

"Never heard of any relatives, or anyone close, but that's not something I'd have heard." Thoughts chased themselves through my mind. Did I know anyone close to Royse? "It's a long shot, but let me call someone. Might be able to find out."

I grabbed my phone and scrolled to Luke's number. This time, I didn't bother going outside. The conversation wouldn't be related to the Hell Raiders, so it didn't matter who heard. He didn't answer, so I left a message, then went back to the floor plans. Luke would call back as soon as he had a training break.

In the meantime, I needed to know everything I could find out about Royse's building. "Let's look floor-by-floor, memorize that fucker's lair."

Stella nodded and pulled the sheet marked 'BASEMENT' to the top of the pile. Most of the rooms there were labeled Storage or Mechanical. "This all looks innocent, until you think about what could be in those storage rooms." Stella looked around. "You got a pen and paper in this joint, man?"

Juaquin flashed his gold grin. "Course I do. I done tol' you, I'm like a fuckin' boy scout, always prepared." He fished around in a kitchen drawer and came up with a small notepad and one of those free pens everyone steals at the bank.

Stella started scribbling something down in some kind of shorthand. Whatever it was, I sure as hell couldn't read it. "Okay, we have to assume the rooms aren't going to be used as labeled. Can't very well put 'Holding Cell' on a floorplan for a commercial building or private residence. City inspectors would pitch ten kinds of hell over that."

"So far, I follow. But where the hell did you learn to write?" The chance to take a jab at Stella refused to be left alone.

He raised an eyebrow. "Shit, I was supposed to be writing something?"

Juaquin laughed. "You know what we need?"

"A tank?"

"Nah, we need someone who's actually been in there and familiar with it." Dude acted like he'd just given some profound advice.

"Too bad volunteers ain't knocking the door down to help, though."

I gave some serious thought to the drug dealer's words, and a spark of an idea started to grow. "Not yet. But if we get word into the right ears that we're looking for someone, they just might."

Stella straightened and turned to look at me full on.

"You think so?"

I shrugged. "Royse has more enemies than friends. Place that big, if he's actually using it, has to have staff, and people who come and go. He's bound to have pissed off at least one of them."

"Huh. You have a point. So where do we find these people who hate Royse that much?"

He had me there. "I'll have to get back to you on that one."

Juaquin held up a finger. "You know any of the chicks Elena worked with?"

I shook my head. "I wouldn't even know her except she was part of the prize for a fight I won. I've seen a ton of girls working for him, but never paid much attention. Got all I wanted without paying."

Juaquin interrupted with a laugh. "Right, ain't no white boy ever got all the pussy he wants without havin' to pay up front. Bitches be smart like dat."

Stella and I both flipped him off. I decided right then Juaquin might be an okay bastard. Either way, he could be a valuable asset. "Ain't my fault if they have a thing for fighters. Either way, I got a call in to a buddy that might know some names for us."

We spent the next hour going over floor plans, searching for some weakness we could exploit. Finally, my phone rang with Luke's return call. "Hey, you able to talk right now?"

"No, Ryker, Luke isn't able to come to the phone right now. I'll be happy to take a message for you, though."

My blood turned to icicles at the fake cheerfulness of Royse's tone. Fuck! I ended the call, cursing the day the fucker was born.

The others looked up with alarm, and Stella stood with a hand on the butt of his .38. "What?"

"Fucking Royse. He called me back from Luke's phone.

Probably means he had his goons beat the poor bastard down, or worse." I ran a hand over my head. "Fuck this. I'm going to get Elena now."

Stella grabbed me as I started for the door. "Wait, Ryker. You could be walking right into a fucking shooting gallery."

I shook him off and went on, not wanting to hurt a Brother if I didn't have to. "I can't leave her in that sick fuck's hands one minute longer." A fresh chill ran along my spine at the thought of the bastard touching her. I had tried to keep my mind from going there, but too late now.

My phone rang again, but I ignored it. I had nothing to say to the fucker. Juaquin's door succeeded in slowing me down for a few seconds, and as I cleared it, Stella's phone went off. I ignored his shout to wait and headed for his car in a sprint.

I slowed, a handful of strides from the car, and something plowed into me from the side, taking me to the ground. I came back up immediately, grateful for all the hours of training. It looked like the fucker had brought the fight to me.

The guy who took me down had a good fifty pounds and several inches on me. I backed up a little to gain a second to check that no more thugs lurked around to come to his defense. Certain no rescuers waited, I moved in, ready to take him apart.

He threw both hands up, fear spreading over his face. "Wait! Wait, man, Juaquin an' Stella say tell you hol' up a minute."

I growled. "What the *fuck*?"

"I'm sorry, man. Juaquin call and say stop you, him an' Stella gotta tell you sum'n 'fore you take off." The guy took another half step back with every word.

Stella raced around the corner before I could say anything more, stopping in front of me with one hand up while he heaved for air. When he finally managed to speak, he still sounded badly winded. "Fuck, man, warn me before I have to chase you down. Smokin' two packs a day ain't good with this fitness shit."

"What the fuck, Stella? This shit ain't cool." It took all my self-control not to take his head for this bullshit.

He took another deep breath. "Sorry, brother. Boss called. Him and the rest of the boys are just a few minutes out."

I shrugged. "And you stopped me for that? I could have done been there, damn it."

"He said it's club business now, and don't go in without backup. They got something about that interference, and he's loaded for war."

Again, I shrugged. "I don't give a fuck. I can't wait for him to get his ass here and more coming up with plans shit." I turned for the car.

"Brother, you know I can't let you go in there against his say-so."

The world slowed down while I turned back to face Stella, the barrel of his .38 steady on my chest. "What. The. Fuck. He tell you to throw down on me?"

He stayed silent for ten heartbeats. "Yeah, brother, he did. Said stop you."

I've taken some serious fucking hits in the cage, but nothing could have floored me like that. "What now?" All I could do was wait for an opening. I might be down for the count, but I sure as fuck wasn't beaten.

Chapter Twenty-Four

Elena:

"Ryker!" His name left my lips on a gasp as I woke.

"I should have known you were cheating on me." The whisper slid through the dim room and squeezed all the air from my lungs.

"What?" I sat up and scooted back against the pillows, and tried to shake sleep off at the same time. "No!" A dark shape loomed over me, like something out of a nightmare. Was that it? Was I just dreaming? I forced my eyes open, trying to see more clearly.

Royse stood over me, scowling down, a fist drawn back. "By the time I'm done with you, your boyfriend won't want to look at you."

Terror hit, and then self-preservation kicked in. "What do you mean? You're my boyfriend." I hated the words. The thought of being involved with anyone other than Ryker seemed crazy wrong. But I had to say them. If I died here, I would never get back to Ryker.

"Bullshit. You lied." He came closer, snarling. "I should kill you." His fist flew and glanced off my cheekbone.

I dodged back, wincing as pain exploded through my head. "I didn't, Royse, I swear!" Tears stung my eyes, and I tried to blink them back, but as the pain from his blow vibrated through my cheek, I couldn't stop them.

My crying just seemed to make him madder. He growled as he drew back again, and I didn't wait around to try and reason with him any longer. I slid to the far side of the bed, frantic to get away. The blankets grabbed my legs and held me tight for too long, as if they were on his side. His hand snagged in my hair as I finally kicked free and rolled to the floor.

"Get back here, bitch!" He dove across the bed, trying to keep his hold.

I pulled away with all my strength, ignoring the searing pain in my scalp, and not caring that I left a big chunk of my hair in his grasp. Better to lose some hair than let him get his hands on me again. Part of the blanket came with me, wrapping around my ankle just enough to let him get close again. Fear held me frozen for an instant, but then I started scrambling away.

Royse crashed behind me with a roar, and grabbed the bottom of the stupid dress he'd made me wear. Knew I should have taken the damn thing off. I kicked at him and pulled away at the same time. My foot caught his elbow, not hard, but enough to loosen his grip a little.

I spun and pushed up, trying to get my feet under me, but he recovered and made another grab for me. This time, he got a firm hold of the dress and yanked, trying to topple me over.

Determination gave me a little extra strength, and I fought not to fall into his grasp. A scream tore from my throat as I hung there, halfway to my feet, struggling for balance. A ripping sound filled the air, and the bottom part of the dress started to tear. I leaned a little harder away from Royse and it tore more. He reached for me with his other hand just as the fabric gave way completely.

I half-fell forward, managing to put a few inches between myself and Royse again. The door seemed like it was miles away, but somehow, I had to get there ahead of him. The slippery floor worked against me, slowing me down. The only good thing was it slowed Royse down, too.

"You will pay for every second of fighting me, cunt. Hell is too good for the likes of you!" He made it to his feet and ran after me, even though I had only gained a few feet on him.

Panic hit again. If he got his hands on me, I would never get away, never see Ryker again, never feel anything but pain again. The room spun as I looked for some weapon, or a way out, or anything that might help.

A fragile looking vase on a tiny table caught my eye and I made a grab for it while I tried to stay ahead of him. Spinning, I threw the heavy vase at him, utterly shocked when the thing hit him.

He gave another furious shout as the vase hit the floor and shattered. "You bitch!"

Fear tried its best to paralyze me, make me stand and wait for him, but I resisted. I toppled the little table in front of him and pushed a few more steps toward the door.

He was gaining on me, reaching for me again. If I didn't do something drastic, he would have me and it would be too late to do anything but pray.

I stopped by the big mirror in the entry and grabbed the gold frame and pulled for all I was worth. For a moment, it seemed like nothing would happen.

Royse stopped to stand right in front of me, grinning like some kind of demented thing from a scary movie. He reached for me, and rather than run, I dragged even harder on that damn mirror.

A splintering noise filled the air, and then suddenly, the mirror came down in slow motion. The bottom edge hit the floor and the top leaned, so I pushed. Glass broke, but it wasn't enough to stop him, and it was too slow.

I pushed harder, until the top of the frame swung toward Royse's head. The mirror's weight started to help at that point, and it fell faster than he could move. Something like fear filled his face as he realized it was going to hit him hard.

As much as I wanted to stay and see if it had any effect, I didn't. I turned and raced once more for the door. The knob turned in my hand and glass broke with a heavy crash behind me. I jerked the door open, not looking back.

In the corridor, Mr. Green headed for me at a run. "Miss? Is everything okay?"

"No! He's trying to kill me!" I pushed past him, desperate to get to the elevator.

He grabbed my arm. "No, come on, this way. He can stop the elevator."

The words sank in past my panic and I allowed Mr. Green to lead me on at a run until we reached a door marked Maintenance. He grabbed it open, shoved me through and pulled the door closed. The only sound I could really hear came from my heart, as it beat so wildly my pulse drowned out anything else.

"This way." He led me behind a shelf filled with cleaning supplies, and another door slid open. "He won't be able to stop this one. Come on." Mr. Green went first into the more modern elevator, hurrying to push the button for the first floor.

With no need to run, or fear for my life, for just a second, my brain started trying to work again. "Why are you helping me?" Was he really? Or was he just playing along with Royse's sick game?

He took a deep breath as the elevator dinged to signal a different floor. "Because I know what kind of monster he is. I can't sit by and let him do this to another girl. You have to get out and tell everyone what he is."

"He's not going to let me go. He still has my mom, and he'll use that." The sobs threatened to start again and I paused to swallow hard. "It's useless to try."

"Shh. Your mom is already safe. We moved her while he was out."

My heart stood still. "What?"

"Look, we—the other people who work here, and I— have seen this before. I've lost count of the number of girls he's done this to. He rescues them in some way, moves them upstairs, and acts as if they're his fiancé. Sooner, rather than later, it always ends."

"Ends?" The elevator dinged again, startling me.

Mr. Green nodded. "Ends. He's insane. He suddenly realizes the girl isn't happy to be here, and he kills her. Every time." He took my arm as the elevator came to a smooth stop. "Come on. None of the other girls had anyone to care for them, or help them stay out of his reach. You do. We're not letting him kill you." He led me at a half-run down the hall a ways, then opened a door. "Mr. Black will take you the rest of the way."

I spun to find Mr. Black watching me with kind eyes. The door closed before I could thank Mr. Green. "What next?"

A huge commotion sounded in the hall, and something heavy banged into the door. I jumped, fresh terror filling me. And somewhere, above all the noise, Royse shouted and cursed.

Mr. Black touched my arm, startling me again. "Here. Climb in." His hoarse whisper seemed overly loud in the small space. He pointed me toward a big wire basket on wheels filled with what looked like sheets and blankets, maybe some tablecloths. "You're going down to the laundry. Mrs. Blue is waiting for you there."

The nod I gave him probably looked braver than I felt. I climbed over the side of the basked, suddenly aware of how little of my dress I still wore. Sinking down, I covered myself with the stuff around me, and waited.

The basket started to move with a jolt and a mechanical groan, and I tried to brace myself without moving or making myself visible to anyone who happened to see. Several jolts and a sickening plunge later, the cart stopped moving. I held my breath and waited.

The fabric above me rustled, as if someone were pulling it aside, and I braced myself for the blow I knew was about to come.

"Now, now, Miss Kitty. You know you're not to be in the linens." The cheery female voice startled the hell out of me. The soft *meow* that followed came as even more of a surprise. A *cat*? "You sit tight, there, Miss. You're safe now, just some waiting to do." Shoes squeaked on the floor as she hurried away.

Well, what was I supposed to do with that? She said wait. Did I dare take her at her word? Hell, did I even know how to actually trust someone? Yeah, come to think of it, I trusted Ryker. Maybe I could take the next step and count on someone who gently scolded cats and put everything on the line to help a stranger she'd never even seen before. So, I sat there, and waited. And waited.

All the cuts and bruises I accumulated as I tried to escape Royse ached and burned with a vengeance, reminding me of their presence with every heartbeat. My right eye seemed swollen nearly shut, and throbbed like hell. I probed it with gentle fingers, not shocked to find a gash that could probably use a stitch or two along my cheekbone.

Worse, doubt came at me from everywhere. How did I know these people were really helping? I couldn't be sure what Mr. Green said about Ryker was true, either. Maybe if I ran now, I could get away on my own. I almost tried it. Almost. But I ended up staying put, relying on others to keep me safe. I figured they were my best chance of escape, even if Ryker wasn't there.

Hours passed and my stomach rumbled, reminding me of the food I'd left on my tray at lunch. Oh well, it wasn't the first time I'd been a little hungry. In the past week, I ate enough to last me a normal month, or more. Missing a meal sure as hell wouldn't hurt me, especially since having something to eat every day had become an outrageous luxury the last few years.

Occasionally, some noise startled me a little, but I forced

myself to stay put, even while every instinct screamed to get the hell out and run for my life. About the time I thought my damn bladder was about to bust, the squeaky footsteps came back. "Okay, Miss, you can come out now. It's safe."

I stayed put. How could I be okay if I was still inside Royse's building?

"Miss, you awake?" The blankets and stuff above me were pulled away. "Ah, there you are." Kind blue eyes peered at me over the edge of the giant basket. "I'm Mrs. Blue. Come on out of there, you must be stiff as a board. Let's get you a drink." She turned away.

I still didn't move.

She came back. "It's okay, darlin'. Himself is busy and won't have time to look for you any time soon. Your friends did a good job getting his attention elsewhere."

Chapter Twenty-Five

Ryker:

I stared at Stella as rage flowed through me. That motherfucker would die for betraying me like this. Especially for claiming it was at Kellen's order. I knew my Prez. He wouldn't call for this, not knowing my woman's life hung in the balance.

Stella gestured with his gun. "Get in the car, brother. We have to go meet the others." He gave me a scowl when I stayed put. "What, you don't want to get your woman back? Changed your mind all of a sudden?"

"What?"

"Just get the fuck in, man, and drive. I'll tell you where. We have to meet the others before it starts going down."

"Fine." I could always stand still and get shot later, after I knew what was going on. I got in and Stella slid into the passenger seat.

"We're going to the warehouse on Water Street. The boys will meet us there."

Before I got the fucking beater running well enough to go anywhere, the back door opened and Juaquin dove inside. "Ya'll didn't forget that promise you made, did you? 'Cause ain't no fucking way Royse goes down without me there."

I rolled my eyes and put the car in gear. "I don't give a shit, as long as you stay the fuck out of my way."

Juaquin laughed. "Likewise, motherfucker."

All my attention shifted to driving, and getting to that warehouse on Water Street as fast as possible. Stella's car succeeded in pissing me off even more with its sluggish responses. Every single time I had a clear way to make up some time, the thing bogged down like it had paste running through the fuel line. The way the engine knocked and shuddered kept me on edge, expecting it to go up in smoke at any second.

I avoided the business district in the interest of time, knowing the traffic would be heavier there, and cut through a quiet residential neighborhood instead. A dog ran across the street and I let off the gas a little in reflex, in case it turned back, or another followed. Instead, a kid darted from between two parked cars. I stomped the brake pedal, and my heart sank as a metal-on-metal grind came from the wheels.

"The fucking brakes are gone?" If I had time, I would jerk Stella out of the car and beat him to a pulp. Instead, I concentrated on getting the damn car to slow enough to miss that kid. By some miracle, the kid ran back out of the street, and we missed him. "What the fuck, Stella?"

Stella looked shaken. "Don't make sense. I checked it all over less than a month ago. Brake pads were worn, but not bad."

"How long you had this piece of shit?"

"I don't know, maybe six or eight weeks. Picked it up for five hundred bucks."

Juaquin laughed his ass off, and I shook my head. "You know how seriously fucked up that is? You pick a ride to keep from drawing attention. Nothing flashy or memorable. I get that. But damn, this fucking cage draws more attention than my car does. In a bad way."

"What the fuck ever, man. Just drive. We're late." Stella waved off my insults about his ride the same as he always did. He acted as if I'd forgotten about him pulling a fucking gun on me.

As I drove, and tried to get us to the warehouse in one piece, I pushed back my anger at Stella. I would deal with him later, after Elena was safe. And no doubt, he knew it was coming. Throwing down a Brother was not a move to make lightly.

The warehouse drew into view, looking like it always did. Situated in the oldest part of town, near the River, the area had recently become popular with college students and young professionals. When Kellen picked up the warehouse for back taxes a few years ago, he had planned to use the rundown building as temporary storage. That quickly changed after several offers from developers. Now the building sat empty, in the process of being renovated and updated. It was going to become a legit income source for the club with a series of nice rental units on one side, and studio apartments on the other.

But for the moment, it offered an ideal space to meet up without drawing too much notice. I pulled around the side, where one of the big rollup doors waited open, and drove right inside. The door went down immediately behind the car. I got the damn thing stopped, put it in Park, shut it off, and climbed out. The only light came from the headlights of the nearly two dozen motorcycles sitting to one side.

Kellen came forward, hand outstretched. "Ryker, good to see you whole, brother."

I nodded and clasped his hand, as usual. "Good to be whole. Had my doubts of surviving that piece of shit Stella calls a car."

Kellen barked with laughter, then shut it off in that eerie way of his. "Look, man, I'm sorry I had him stop you. Don't blame him for it, all on me. There was no choice, though. New info about our interference problem came in, and you could have walked right into a shooting gallery." His eyes widened as he looked over my shoulder. "Who the fuck is that?"

I turned as Juaquin climbed out of the back of Stella's jalopy. "That's Juaquin. Elena's neighbor, and the man with the floor plans to Royse's building." I motioned the guy forward. "Juaquin, Kellen."

The two shook hands cautiously. "Anything you see or hear today stays with you, yeah? Hate to have my boys pay you a visit to remind you to keep your trap shut."

"No prob'm, homes. Same here. Don't want my bidness spread all over fuck and back."

I winced as I rolled my shoulder. "Take my word for it, boss, his boys pack a punch. Now can we get shit moving? I ain't gettin' no younger."

Fabio and Crank came forward, and Fabio spoke first. "So, we followed up with what you and Stella got on your little trip, and found a low-life that knew about Royse's deal with those boys down there." Since we had company, the ex-Marine took care not to reveal names or locations, exactly as if he were talking on an unsecured phone.

Crank put in his two cents. "We started doing our thing, following the trail, and we found where Royse stores the goods he's selling. Bastard couldn't settle for being a middleman. He wanted the whole fucking enchilada."

The whole dog and pony show sparked nothing but my impatience. "And?"

"He keeps the shit in his building. Nobody would think to look at a nice, historic place like that. And the fucker lives right there with the goods."

As badly as I wanted to get moving, I knew we needed a plan of some sort. "What are we doing then?"

Kellen and Fabio spent the next fifteen minutes outlining the simple plan and making sure everyone had as many weapons as they could carry. Our information had expired, so we had no way of knowing what sort of inventory Royse sat on, or how many men he had there. That meant we were going in expecting to face an army. Especially since Crank had been able to confirm Royse's connection to some Russian criminals associated with the bunch we'd tangled with before.

Finally, we got moving, and left the warehouse a few at

a time, from different exits. The old building was ideally situated for our purpose. If Raiders' operations ever expanded substantially to the area, it could make a good front for storage. People could have their nice little apartments, and we could leave a few units empty to store our shit. But, no doubt, Kellen had already considered that option. I put it out of mind, and concentrated on getting to Elena and getting her out of Royse's hands.

Doubt hit again as I rode shotgun in Stella's beater. Did Elena even want away from Royse? Hell, the man had taken her mom in, got her a doctor, and Juaquin said she was wearing nice clothes. What the fuck did I have to offer her, compared to all that? All I had was myself. It didn't seem like such a great tradeoff to me.

Would she have any interest in leaving the guy that could give her everything she never had, and going with the one that had a bike, a muscle car and a rented apartment? If she was smart, no. But that wasn't going to stop me from trying. By this point, I couldn't even consider life without Elena in it, so I had to do everything possible to get her to leave him.

The Hell Raiders arrived at Royse's building in waves, taking up our assigned positions on all sides, and waited. After a short time, Royse himself left in a hurry, presumably to deal with the trouble Crank and Fabio had cooked up at the abandoned factory where the illegal fights took place.

We waited some more, to give Royse time to reach the old factory so the rest of the team could take care of him. The sun dropped for the horizon, leaving us in the low light before twilight.

And then, Kellen gave the signal to move in.

I headed for the side door, as planned, with Dix at my side. We didn't bother trying to stay out of sight any more. When twenty bikers broke cover and jogged for the doors with guns out and ready, whoever was inside knew without a doubt something was happening.

The door consisted mostly of wood, with a thick frosted glass window. I didn't even hesitate. The window shattered under the butt of my .45, and I reached through and quickly found the lock mechanism. Seconds later, Dix and I made our way inside.

Chapter Twenty-Six

Elena:

Friends? What friends did I have? I asked myself a million and one questions as I followed orders and climbed out of the basket. Mrs. Blue supported me as my legs wobbled and threatened to dump me on the floor.

"Is there a bathroom?" As much as I needed to get away, out of Royse's reach forever, at the moment, I needed the bathroom worse.

"Oh, of course! I'm sorry, I should have realized." Middle aged and round, Mrs. Blue gave me a kind smile and led the way. When I came out of the tiny, but spotless, bathroom, Mrs. Blue waited with a bundle of clothing. "I thought you might need these, Miss. I'll get you a drink and something to eat while you get changed."

The remnants of Royse's dress fell away and I hurried to put on the track pants and hoodie, then the sneakers. By the time I finished tying the laces, Mrs. Blue came back.

"It isn't much, Miss, but it should hold you until you can get somewhere else." She passed over a sandwich wrapped in wax paper, and a canned soda.

"Thanks, it's perfect." I opened the drink immediately and took a gulp to sooth my parched throat. "Can you tell me what's going on?" The paper crinkled as I unwrapped the sandwich and took a bite.

"I don't have all the details, Miss. Just that Mr. Green spoke with someone who knew of your situation, and they asked for help getting you out. We all agreed to help. So now, you're in the staff lounge, in the basement, and we're waiting for your friends to show up." She spoke as if I knew all this already.

"I don't understand. No one really knows I'm here." The food hit my system and I realized how sluggish my brain had been before.

"Well, it seems someone does, and he wants you out."

"And what about my mom?" I took another bite and waited. They'd said she was already safe, but I needed some sort of confirmation, I guess.

"Oh, we moved her already. While he was gone in the afternoon, she left with a load of furnishings that were bound for storage. A friend met the truck and took her to a safe place where she'll be taken care of until it's safe for you to contact her." The kindly woman offered a smile as she fidgeted a little.

It didn't make sense. "Why are you and the others taking such a big risk for me? I don't understand."

"Oh, Miss, we know the kinds of things that go on here. None of us likes it one bit. Until now, we've been unable to help, though. With your friends ready to get you away and keep you safe, we're also safe. He need never know we hid you until they could come for you." She smiled again, looking as pleased as the cartoon cat that ate the little yellow bird. "It's our one chance to right some of the wrongs we've bore witness to."

I still had my doubts, but right then, I didn't want to question her kindness any further. If I made her mad, she might just hand my ass right back over to Royse. "Thank you for helping." It would be nice to know who the friends were she kept mentioning. That part worried me even more.

As I finished my sandwich and drink, a lot of noise echoed through the basement.

"Ah, there they are, right on schedule." She looked even more pleased with herself. "Come along, I'll show you to the exit." She took my soda can and sandwich wrapper and disposed of them, then opened a door I hadn't noticed before.

"This way."

I followed Mrs. Blue down a narrow hall, my heart threatening to choke me at every step. For all I knew, this woman could be leading me right back to an extremely pissed off Royse. All I had to go on was her story, and I'd learned long ago not to trust anyone at their word. People all had their own plans, and put their own spin on whatever came out of their mouths, and it rarely went the way anyone claimed.

We reached a solid metal door at the end of the hall, and I held my breath as Mrs. Blue shoved it open. Nobody waited to kill me, though, so I followed her through and down another hall. The noise from earlier grew louder, and I could make out shouts, and what seemed like the bang of doors being kicked in.

At a second door, Mrs. Blue paused with her finger over her lips, signaling for quiet. Apparently satisfied, she turned back to me. "Okay, Miss, I can't go any further. Out this door and up one set of stairs. One of your friends is meant to be waiting, but just in case they're not, the door to your right will lead you outside the building. To your right and around the corner is the front entrance." She leaned in for a quick hug, startling me. "Be safe, Miss."

I returned her hug after a second. "Thank you, Mrs. Blue. Tell Mr. Green and Mr. Black I said thanks to them. I would be dead now without all your help."

"Think nothing of it, Miss. Just live a safe, happy life." She pulled the heavy door open and waved me through.

The noises were far louder now, but I still couldn't make out words, or tell for sure what the loud bangs were. Shaking like a leaf and scared to death, I crept up the stairs, practically feeling my way, since the only light filtered down from above.

"Shh! You hear something?" The voice came from somewhere ahead. I froze in my tracks and tried to melt into the rough concrete steps.

"Nah, man, you're hearing stuff."

"No, I'm not. Shut the fuck up." The harsh whisper sounded slightly familiar.

I stayed put, trying to get my heart under control before they heard it pounding against my ribs.

The first voice came again. "Shit, man, where the hell is she? It's five minutes late."

"Calm down, Ryker, she'll show."

Ryker?

Chapter Twenty-Seven

Ryker:

Right now, I hated Kellen. When we got to Royse's building, the fucker went all cloak and dagger on me, and sent Dix and me to cool our fucking heels in an empty stairwell. Supposedly, someone would bring Elena to me there, but they were late. I was so amped, I could punch a truck-sized hole in a brick wall, but Dix kept trying to talk me down.

I'd had enough. "Fuck this. I ain't standing here waiting while Elena could be any damn where in this hell hole."

Another small sound caught my attention, this time loud enough that I caught the direction. Someone was below us, on the next level of the stairs. I held up a finger to let Dix know, and he nodded. He'd heard it, too.

Guns drawn, we spread out and crept around the railing.

I caught the faint gleam of light on red hair. "Elena!" I leaped down the stairs to clutch her to me. "Are you okay?"

She nodded a little. "I am now."

"Let's get you out of here." I swung her up into my arms and took the stairs two at a time. Ahead of me, Dix watched to clear the way, then held the outer door open for me. Outside, I ran with her to Stella's damned old car, praying the heap would get us at least far enough to keep her safe.

I climbed in the back with Elena still in my arms while Dix took the driver's seat. The car gave a sluggish groan, but finally the engine turned over. I held my breath until Royse's building was out of sight.

"Where we going, Ryker?" Dix's words brought my mind back into the game.

"My place." I gave directions. Now that I could breathe again, I took a moment to put a soft kiss on Elena's lips. She gasped a little, and I looked at her more closely. Her face was battered and swollen. "What the hell did that bastard do to you?" Rage surged through me.

"I-I'm okay. It looks worse than it is." She lowered her gaze, nervously tucking a strand of hair behind her ear. "It doesn't matter now."

I studied each mark on her beautiful skin. "Yeah, it matters. The fucker put his hands on you."

She put one hand against my cheek, and I leaned into it like a puppy looking for pats. Fucking pathetic, but I didn't care. "No, Ryker, all that matters is I'm with you now. Nothing else." Her words reached into my chest and grabbed my heart.

I smiled a little. "You're right. Nothing else matters." I let my lips ease along hers, careful not to hurt her. "I've got you, baby girl." I pulled her into my lap, vowing nothing would take her from my arms ever again.

When we reached my building, I sent Dix back to the others with my bike, and helped Elena into the Chevelle. I agreed wholeheartedly with this part of the plan. Elena stayed quiet as we drove out of town, and I didn't push for conversation. I needed to concentrate on making sure we weren't followed, and I couldn't very well do that if I was all absorbed in her.

Once we crossed the bridge, I put the miles behind us in a hurry. "Are you doing okay?" I needed to know more than I could have imagined.

She took a shaky breath. "I am now."

"Good." I drove on in silence for a bit. Then I asked for, and she gave, details about what went on while she was with Royse.

"He was insane. I hope your friends killed him." I sensed her shudder on the other side of the seat.

Time to change the subject. "Elena? I know you left to try and help your mom, and to keep me safe. Thank you." Even if her plan didn't work, I owed her gratitude.

A bitter little laugh filled the car. "I didn't do such a great job at either, and just made more trouble for you."

I thought about her words for a moment. "Partly. But you also made me think. A lot." I took a deep breath, trying to get my nerve up. "At first, I was pissed and ready to just walk away. But then I realized I didn't want to do that. In fact, I figured out I wanted to keep you around for a long time."

"You did?" Her voice sounded small and fragile.

"I did." I reached for her hand and drew it to my lips to kiss her knuckles. "Try to rest a little. We'll be there soon and things will be busy for a while." Her hand felt so small and fragile in mine, and I cradled it carefully and didn't let go.

When we arrived at the clubhouse, Georgie, Dix's ol' lady, and Tonya, Trip's ol' lady, were waiting for us. They whisked Elena away, and made clear I wasn't welcome, sending me to hang out with Badger until the others came back.

I grabbed a beer from the fridge and joined the old codger in front of the TV, where the local news showed headlines from local sports. "Hey, old man."

"Hey yourself, kid. So you finally got your head out of your ass and took your woman back, huh?" Leave it to Badger to put things clearly.

"Yeah, guess so." Where the hell did he hear that?

"Bout damn time. Never seen such a hard-headed bunch as you young'uns. In my day, if we seen a woman we wanted, we didn't waste no time." He drained his beer and immediately grabbed another from a small cooler beside his chair.

I chose to ignore him, and drank some more of my own beer. By the time I took the last swallow, the roar of bikes coming up the lane brought me to my feet. Kellen and several other Raiders came in, looking dog tired. I stood and waited to hear what had gone on at Royse's building.

"You got her home okay, brother?"

"I did. She's with Georgie and Tonya now. They wouldn't let me tag along." I realized I sounded more than a little whiny, and didn't even give a fuck.

Kellen laughed. "Probably for the best, man." He slapped me on the shoulder and went to grab beer from the fridge, passing them around to the others. Everyone dropped into chairs, clearly glad for the beer.

"Thanks, boys. To another successful operation." Kellen raised his bottle to the room in general. "We shut down the interference, added some inventory, and helped Ryker get his woman back."

"Thanks, brothers, I appreciate you all sticking your necks out to help me get Elena safe. And her mom, too." I lifted my fresh beer to them.

Elena came in with Georgie and Tonya, and a couple of the club girls. I froze, staring at her. She still bore the bruises and cuts of her last encounter with Royse. And despite all that, she was still the most beautiful woman in the whole fucking world.

Breathless, I stood and waited as she wove her way through the chairs, not looking in either direction. Finally, she came within reach. I stretched my arms out and pulled her to me, wanting nothing more than to hold her forever. Instead, I leaned in to kiss her like a man starving for a mere taste.

All around, my Brothers whooped and clapped.

I drew back a little, smiling against Elena's mouth. "Ready to get out of here?"

She nodded shyly, allowing me to tuck her against my side.

"Night, brothers, and thank you again." I led her toward the hall and my room amid more whoops and cheers. Elena flushed, and I flipped them off over my shoulder. I dug my keys out and opened the door to my room, flipping the light on. "Welcome to my home away from home."

She paused just inside the door, looking shy and unsure of herself.

A sudden thought hit me. "If you'd rather, I can find you another room. I don't want you to feel pressured, or anything."

To my surprise, she looked up at me with wide, dark eyes, and her lower lip trembled a little. "Is that what you want?"

I ran my hands over my head. "Baby girl, I want you in my arms. It doesn't have to go further than that. I just want to be near you."

Horrified, I watched as two big tears rolled over her lashes. Suddenly, she threw herself into my arms, wound her own around my neck, and pulled me down to her level. The kiss she gave me said so much more than words could manage.

She told me everything I needed to know as her lips clung to mine, and her tongue danced with mine. Every bit of fear came through, along with her desire and need to be close to me. Hopes for a future she never dreamed about followed. I gave it all back to her, hoping she understood.

My lungs threatened to implode with the need for air before I drew back. "Are you okay?" I needed to know for sure, before I asked her to go further.

"I need you, Ryker. Make love to me." She stepped back a little and stripped off her hoodie, revealing naked tits that my hands ached for.

Hungry to have her skin on mine, I ditched my shirt as fast as I could peel it off, and stepped in close. Hard nipples brushed against my chest in time with her breathing, and my jeans suddenly went from snug to strangling.

"Get everything else off for me?" I kicked my boots off and practically ripped my jeans open.

She gave a nod, and her clothes quickly joined mine on

the floor. She stood there before me, a little shy and unsure, but eager.

"Fucking beautiful." I pulled her to me and bent to kiss her tenderly. The bruises and scrapes marring her smooth skin made me furious, but for now, that took second place to my need for her. I scattered careful kisses over her face, wanting to soothe every bruise.

Elena sighed, her breath feathering against my shoulder, and her hands skimmed up my ribs. I cupped her jaw to angle her head perfectly for my kiss, and once more tasted her lips. Her soft moan encouraged me, and I let my other hand trail down her spine to the upper curve of her ass. She stepped back, her hands dropping to my hips to pull me after her as she backed toward the bed.

"Hold that thought for a second." I reached around her to pull the blankets back. "I want my baby girl on clean sheets, not a dusty blanket." Satisfied, I lifted her and settled her gently in the middle of the bed. "I'm starved for you, Elena."

Her thighs fell open to make room for me, and I lowered my shoulders between her knees. The little whimper she gave when she felt my breath on her pussy sent my need for her into overdrive. I spread her wide, licking and tasting like a starving man.

She moaned and sank her fingers into my hair, pulling me tighter to her. No need to ask twice. I put my arm across her belly to hold her, and feasted on her, fucking her with my tongue until she writhed and bucked against me. The muscles of her belly tightened with the beginnings of her orgasm. I flattened my tongue over her clit and slipped a finger inside her, stroking deep.

She came apart, crying out and trembling. I let her catch her breath, then made my way up her body, kissing and licking every curve. When I reached her mouth, she moaned and arched her hips against me. My hard-on slipped between her wet folds to stroke her clit, and her nails raked down my shoulders in response.

Elena shifted a little, hooking her legs around my waist. I poised for a second to enjoy how she quivered with my cock at her entrance, then sank home. Her inner muscles clenched around me as I withdrew.

Over and over, I drove into her, and every time she met my thrusts eagerly. The sensations of being inside her threatened to entirely overwhelm my senses, and I stilled to try and maintain control.

She refused to allow it, though, arching and wriggling her hips, milking my cock. "Don't stop, baby, I'm too close."

At her urging, I drove into her again, faster and faster, while my orgasm built at the base of my spine.

"I love you." Her body contracted, pulling me deeper as she fell to pieces once more.

Her words sank in, and drove me over the edge. "I love you." The realization of what I'd said hit hard. I never used those words, but with her, they were natural. And true. "Don't you ever leave me again, baby girl. I want you with me, always."

"Always?" She sounded terrified, her voice small and careful.

I shifted my weight off her and drew her to my side. I should probably have given some deep thought about my feelings, but I didn't need to. "Elena, I know we don't know each other all that well, and it's really fast, but I want time with you. I want more. Will you be my ol' lady?" I held my breath while she processed the question.

"You're talking about a relationship? Not me being a whore for the club?" Her voice still held that small, scared tone.

"I'm not sharing you, Elena." I turned so I could see her face. "You're mine. As my ol' lady, you'll be treated with respect and care by everyone in the club. You'll be safer than the gold in Fort Knox. I'll cherish you, love you, and be faithful to you." I took a deep breath, aware of the depth of commitment I offered. And I'd never wanted anything more in my life.

She smiled up at me. "I'd like that."

We would have to work out the details, of course, but we could do it. Emotion filled my chest and tightened my throat as I touched my lips to hers. "You want to give it a go?"

She nodded. "Yeah, I do."

Her words left me torn between the need to shout the news from the rooftop, and the need to lose myself in her body once more. I bent to kiss her more deeply, choosing to show her how happy her choice made me.

THE END

Keep reading! If you enjoyed Prizefight,

please remember to leave a review.

Here's Chapter One of *Kellen's Redemption*, Book 1 of the Hell Raiders MC series.

KELLEN'S REDEMPTION

By

Aden Lowe

A HELL RAIDERS MC

ROMANCE

Thank you for purchasing an authorized copy of this book. By doing so, you say NO to Piracy and support authors so they can continue to bring you the books you enjoy.

Author's Note: This book contains adult situations and language, violence, and sexual activity. Mature readers only.

Acknowledgements:

A lot of people made this book possible. First, my wife, Elyse. Thank you for your continued support and encouragement, and your faith in my abilities. Mom, thanks for the occasional smack to the head to knock some sense into me. Ashley Wheels, my Assistant/baby sister...what can I say except thank you for being you. You put up with my weirdness, keep me focused and on track even when it means ten-minute check-ins for hours on end, and you constantly encourage me to do my best. You handle all the frustrating details, put my marketing plans in place, and contribute ideas and suggestions daily. Thank you. Team, remember?

Aden Lowe's Huntresses are the BEST Street Team on Facebook or anywhere else. Thank you ladies for your enthusiastic support. I'm still amazed that you're willing to spend some of your precious down-time helping me. You kick ass.

The Lowe-Down – the Official Aden Lowe Fan Group... Thank you ladies. I rely on you for laughs, opinions, and help promoting my books. You constantly excel in all categories.

All the bloggers who selflessly promote my work, and that of other Indie Authors... You are amazing and without you, the book world would stall out and cease to turn. Thank you!

I sincerely hope you enjoy reading Kellen's Redemption. This book is one of those rare ones that just happened. After you read it, I hope you'll take a moment to leave an honest review on Amazon and/or Goodreads.

If you enjoyed Kellen's Redemption, you might also like my Hunted Love series:

Chapter One - Two Weeks Ago

Kellen came awake fast and pushed away the sweaty sheets. Fucking smokes were too far away. He sat up with a groan, squinting against the monster head-ache eating his brain. Finally got the cigarette free of the pack, in his mouth and lit. The JD Black bottle beside the bed still held half a mouthful, and he snatched it up in relief, swallowed, then wished for more. Considered falling back into bed and sleeping the rest of the day away. No, he had business to handle.

Not bothering to cover up the morning wood, he stumbled out of the room and into the dark hallway and four doors down to where the bathroom stood open. A healthy piss later, he turned the shower on and stepped under the scalding spray. The filth from the last twenty-four hours took some convincing, but finally gave up and went down the drain. Road dirt was the easy part. The stains on his conscience for the part he'd played in that debacle out west would take a while to fade. He scrubbed harder. He'd done far worse, so why did he give a damn?

Feeling somewhat human, he halfway toweled off and went back to his room long enough to pull on his jeans and boots. Back out in the hall, something almost smelled good. One of the old ladies must be up and about, feeling domestic. He followed his nose to the kitchen out of sheer curiosity.

In the big kitchen, Tanya, Trip's old lady, stood over the stove. She glanced over her shoulder, cautious as always, then relaxed visibly when she realized it was Kellen. "Have a seat. It'll be ready in a couple minutes."

Kellen followed orders and dropped into the chair at the head of the big dining table. "Why you cooking?" Some of the old ladies liked to cook when they were at the house, but usually in the mornings someone just made coffee and breakfast was whatever you could find.

Movements guarded, she lifted one shoulder. "Figured you guys might want to start the day on a full belly." A survivor of slavery in another MC, Tanya was careful about everything she did or said. She'd only just become slightly comfortable with Kellen, and only because he didn't bother to take enough notice of her to be intimidating.

He grunted. "Thanks. Smells good." Hmph. Good thing none of the boys heard that. They'd think he'd gone soft. The President of an outlaw motorcycle club did not thank another guy's old lady for anything.

Tanya ignored the slip and went on with what she was doing, leaving Kellen to his thoughts. Eventually, she reached for plates and dished up what she'd cooked. "Here you go." She deposited a plate in front of Kellen, and turned to pour coffee, placing it beside him.

Keeping himself in check, Kellen nodded his thanks, and dug in. Burritos filled with scrambled eggs, sausage and peppers, smothered in a cheese sauce. "This is good." Back inside his head, he ate methodically, preoccupied with the upcoming day. He had to take care of some business.

Hack, his VP, shuffled in, fully dressed and looking like hell had eaten him for breakfast and puked him back up. Old boy was partying too hard lately, and it showed. He dropped into a chair and scrubbed his hands over his face. Tanya, smart girl that she was, slid a plate and coffee in front of him before he could look up. The bastard had a rep for being rough on women. Hell, even his name said it. In the middle of a party at the clubhouse, a girl had been going down on him and he'd shoved his dick so far in her throat she started coughing and hacking. Frustrated that he couldn't finish, he'd backhanded her off him and stomped out. From then on, he was known as Hack.

"What the fuck is wrong with you?"

Rather than answer, Hack shoved his plate aside and pulled a cellophane packet from his jeans. He'd used the outer wrapper from a cigarette pack and sealed a pill inside by melting the end with a lighter. With the obsessive care of a long-time addict, he laid out his pill, lighter, card and straw, pulled a new cellophane off his cigarettes to cover his pill before crushing it down. More careful ritual as he cut and snorted his first line. "You want to bump it?"

Kellen shook his head. "Lay off that shit, man. I need you clear headed." For the millionth time, he wished the club had chosen a different VP, someone who didn't constantly chase the next pill. Hack was a good, solid Brother, but he wasn't VP material.

"You need me able to fucking move." He hit the rest of the pill and put his shit away, making sure to get every last particle of residue off the table. With his day properly started, he grabbed the plate and started eating. "What we got on today?"

"We roll over to that deal later. Nobody but us for this one." Kellen settled back with his coffee.

Hack eyed him, expression cautious. "You sure that's a good idea, boss?"

The empty coffee cup hit the table with a thump as Kellen stood. "Yeah, I am." Understatement. Hack questioning his decision mattered a hell of a lot more. He'd let it slide one time, but the shit couldn't continue.

He headed back to the bathroom and his razor. He looked, and felt, much more human after he'd shaved and trimmed his beard. With his ink, gauged earlobes, and the way he dressed, no one would ever mistake him for a good boy. But they sure as fuck couldn't call him a filthy biker either. Satisfied, he pulled on a t-shirt and his cut, ready to head out.

Back in the kitchen, he came to an impatient halt. "You ready, man? We got shit to tend to."

Hack was just finishing his coffee. "Yeah, yeah." He shoved his chair back and stood, acting stiff and sore as hell.

Probably spent the night fighting or fucking. Dude was getting too old for that shit. Boots thumped on the floor as Hack followed, deliberately making his displeasure known.

Kellen would deal with that shit privately. Outside, the bikes were placed strategically, closest to their owners' most convenient exit from the clubhouse. His own sat outside the window to his room where he could just dive out of bed and hit the leather. The big stretched out chopper started with its usual purr, giving him the thrill of satisfaction. His design, built with his hands. Nothing like it.

Hack rolled up on his '77 Harley Low Rider and gave Kellen a ready nod, so he hit the throttle and headed down the lane. Normally he'd have a couple more guys on a run like this one, but this was a new connection and he needed it kept quiet. So it was just him and Hack, which left him feeling unusually vulnerable.

Nearly an hour on the road and they crossed the River into Ohio. Kellen led them through the run-down residential area of the little town, weaving through the rabbit-warren of alleys and side-streets. Finally, he pulled into a narrow driveway beside a beat-to-death 80-something Lincoln Continental and slipped his bike past it and around to the back of the half boarded-up house.

He parked by the back porch and dismounted and pulled his helmet off as Hack stopped beside him. "Wait here. If it goes sideways, book it out of here."

"Yeah, boss." Hack slid the cut-down twelve gauge out of his jacket and pulled the hammer back, ready for trouble.

Fuck, Kellen hated this kind of shit. The hair stood on the back of his neck as he stepped up onto the creaky old porch. If his middle-man hadn't insisted on the meeting place and vouched for the seller, he wouldn't have considered it. Through the busted down door and a quick step to the side to avoid being silhouetted, everything stayed silent. Kellen strode through the gutted kitchen, his swagger betraying none of his discomfort.

The living room showed no sign of the destruction apparent through the rest of the house. It had been painted, and set up with a couch, a couple of chairs, and a big screen TV, complete with a gaming system.

His guy sat stiffly in one of the chairs, looking like he'd rather be just about anywhere else. On the couch, a woman who belonged on the pages of a glossy magazine sat, sexy bare legs crossed at the knee.

Kellen glared at his guy and mentally crossed him off the 'somewhat trusted' list. "Cheap, I wouldn't be here if you'd mentioned your seller didn't have a dick."

The bitch's immaculately painted lips tightened. "Does it really matter? I have guns, you need guns."

Kellen turned his glare to the perfect features and designer clothing. She had a point. "I'm here now. No sense wasting the trip. Show me what you've got."

She flipped her perfect honey-colored hair back, and opened the leather bag at her side. "What's your poison? Revolvers?" She pulled three revolvers out, different calibers. "Semi-autos? Something with a little more punch?" More than a dozen weapons were laid out on the coffee table before her, ranging from a little .22 derringer to an assault rifle. "I have a truckload, nearly one thousand guns, of which these are a representative sample, all untraceable and clean."

Lit cigarette hanging from his lip, Kellen dropped into the other chair and began to examine the guns. They were all good, and he wanted them, and more. "First, before we talk business, how does a high class whore get in the gun business?"

She raised one elegant brow and straightened her back. "First, I might be high class, but I'm no whore. I fuck for fun, not money." Her golden brown gaze dropped, pausing at his groin, as if assessing him. "And second, not that it's any of your business, but I inherited the gun business. Satisfied?"

His cock twitched in response to her boldness. "Far from it. But I'm on the clock. So talk to me. What terms are you looking for?"

Her tongue slid across her full lower lip, creating a rush of heat through his groin. "In that case, we'll talk again when you're not so busy." She continued, naming her prices for each type of weapon.

After a quick negotiation, they settled on a price they could both live with and made arrangements for delivery and payment. Kellen rose, ready to get the fuck out of the creepy place. He extended a hand to seal the deal.

The woman stood, the top of her head nearly level with his eyes. "Baby, I don't shake on things." She stepped close and leaned up, one perfectly manicured hand going to the back of his neck.

Stunned, Kellen didn't resist, allowing her to pull him down for a kiss. When she licked at the seam of his lips, he opened for her in an uncharacteristic submission. Her tongue swept into his mouth, clearly staking ownership. What the fuck? He woke from the spell with a little growl and took charge. One hand went behind her to grab a handful of her delicious designer ass and drag her to him, while the other sank into all that hair and grasped the back of her skull to tip her head just right.

She hissed when she came into contact with his hard-on, but didn't pull away. Instead, she allowed him to taste and explore, to plunder her mouth.

Kellen finally backed off a little to catch his breath. "How do I reach you so we can finish this?"

She stared up at for a moment. "Your guy there can reach me. Let me know when you're free for a few hours." One hand slid between them to squeeze his cock. "And don't wait too long. I'm anxious to see what kind of weapon you pack." And just like that, she stepped away.

Teaching high-class pussy about the dangers of bad boys

offered a tempting diversion, but no, he had plans. He turned on his heel and left.

***

Pick up your copy of *Kellen's Redemption*

on Amazon!

Check Out My Other Books

Hell Raiders MC Romance Series

Kellen's Redemption (Hell Raiders MC Book #1)
Dixon's Resurrection (Hell Raiders MC Book #2)
Trip's Retribution (Hell Raiders MC Book #3)

Hunted Love Series

Big Game: Hunted Love #1
Bounty : Hunted Love #2
Captured: Hunted Love #3

Ride Series – Co Written with Ashley Wheels

Ride It Out
Ride The Bench – Coming Soon

Connect with me on Facebook or at my website,

www.AdenLowe.com

36218892R00123

Made in the USA
San Bernardino, CA
16 July 2016